## BLOOD GAMBLE

Falconi timed one full minute with the sweep hand of his watch. After exactly sixty seconds he said, "Blow 'em!"

There was one solid second of silence. Then the whole area blasted into a noisy, thunderous, dusty, windy, man-made storm. Pieces of dirt, vegetation and rocks shot through the air with the force of bullets.

"Go for it, guys!" Falconi yelled to the Bravos. He glanced back at the Alphas closing in tight behind them. The desperate looks in the men's eyes showed they fully realized the gamble they were taking.

The chips were in the middle of the table, and the final bet made. There was one last card to play, and it would be dealt by old Mister Death—from his own deck!

## BLACK EAGLES
### by John Lansing

They're the best jungle fighters the United States has to offer. No matter where Charlie is hiding, The Eagles will find him! They're the greatest unsung heroes of the dirtiest, most challenging war of all time!

#1: HANOI HELLGROUND           (1249, $2.95)

#2: MEKONG MASSACRE           (1294, $2.50)

#5: SAIGON SLAUGHTER           (1476, $2.50)

#6: AK-47 FIREFIGHT           (1542, $2.50)

#7: BEYOND THE DMZ           (1610, $2.50)

#8: BOOCOO DEATH           (1677, $2.50)

#9: BAD SCENE AT BONG SON           (1793, $2.50)

#10: CAMBODIA KILL-ZONE           (1953, $2.50)

*Available wherever paperbacks are sold, or order direct from the Publisher. Send cover price plus 50¢ per copy for mailing and handling to Zebra Books, Dept. 1953, 475 Park Avenue South, New York, N.Y. 10016. Residents of New York, New Jersey and Pennsylvania must include sales tax. DO NOT SEND CASH.*

# CAMBODIA KILL-ZONE #10

## THE BLACK EAGLES

### BY JOHN LANSING

**ZEBRA BOOKS**
**KENSINGTON PUBLISHING CORP.**

Special Acknowledgment to: Patrick E. Andrews

ZEBRA BOOKS

are published by

Kensington Publishing Corp.
475 Park Avenue South
New York, NY 10016

First printing: December 1986

Printed in the United States of America

# THE BLACK EAGLES ROLE OF HONOR

(Assigned or Attached Personnel Killed in Action)

*It is a high thing, a bright honor, for a man to do battle with the enemy for the sake of his children, and for his land and his true wife; and death is a thing that will come when the spinning destinies make it come.*

*— Greek lyric posted in the 82nd Airborne Division Museum*

Sgt. Barker, Toby — U.S. Marine Corps
Sgt. Barthe, Eddie — U.S. Army
1st Lt. Blum, Marc — U.S. Air Force
Sgt. Boudreau, Marcel — U.S. Army
Sgt. Carter, Demond — U.S. Army
Staff Sgt. Dayton, Marvin — U.S. Army
Sfc. Galchaser, Jack — U.S. Army
Sgt. Hodges, Trent — U.S. Army
Mr. Hosteins, Bruno — ex-French Foreign Legion
Petty Officer 2nd Class Jackson, Fred — U.S. Navy
Chief Petty Officer Jenkins, Claud — U.S. Navy
Spec. 4 Laird, Douglas — U.S. Army
Sgt. Limo, Raymond — U.S. Army
Petty Officer 3rd Class Littleton, Michael — U.S. Navy
Lt. Martin, Buzz — U.S. Navy
Petty Officer 2nd class Martin, Durwood — U.S. Navy
Staff Sgt. Maywood, Dennis — U.S. Army
Sfc. Miskoski, Jan — U.S. Army
Staff Sgt. Newcomb, Thomas — Australian army

1st Lt. Nguyen Van Dow—South Vietnamese army
Staff Sgt. O'Quinn, Liam—U.S. Marine Corps
Sfc. Ormond, Norman—U.S. Army
Sgt. Park, Chun Ri—South Korean marines
Sfc. Rivera, Manuel—U.S. Army
Master Sgt. Snow, John—U.S. Army
Lt. Thompson, William—U.S. Navy
Staff Sgt. Tripper, Charles—U.S. Army
1st Lt. Wakely, Richard—U.S. Army
Gunnery Sgt. White, Jackson—U.S. Marine Corps
Staff Sgt. Whitaker, George—Australian army

# ROSTER OF THE BLACK EAGLES

(Operation Cambodian Challenge)


Maj. Robert Falconi
*U.S. Army*
Commanding Officer

Lt. Chris Hawkins
*U.S. Navy*
Deputy Commanding Officer

Master Sgt. Duncan Gordon
*U.S. Army*
Operations Sergeant

Sfc. Ray Swift Elk
*U.S. Army*
Intelligence Sergeant

Master Sgt. Chun Kim
*South Korean marines*
Heavy Weapons

Chief Petty Officer Leland Brewster
*U.S. Navy*
Communications Chief

Sfc. Calvin Culpepper
*U.S. Army*
Demolitions Sergeant

Sfc. Malcomb McCorckel
*U.S. Army*
Detachment Medic

Staff Sgt. William Taylor
*Australian army*
Light Weapons

Staff Sgt. Archibald Dobbs
*U.S. Army*
Detachment Scout

Staff Sgt. Enrique Valverde
*U.S. Army*
Supply Sergeant

Petty Officer 3rd Class Blue Richards
*U.S. Navy*
Demolitions

Sgt. Jacob Bernstein
*U.S. Marine Corps*
Light Weapons

# Prologue

The unit's four Soviet M1937 eighty-two-millimeter mortars were laid in and ready. Their target had already been zeroed in, thus the gunners had been able to quickly set elevations and traverse before leveling the bubbles on the MPM-44 sights. Each assistant gunner now held one of the HE rounds, fuzed and ready with the fins resting on the tube bore. They waited impatiently for the order to fire.

Their commanding officer noted the raised hands of the gunners that indicated the readiness of each weapon. He smiled to himself and looked back again toward the target area across the border in South Vietnam. He was standing at the apex of a steep hill, so even without his binoculars the officer could see the wisps of the smoke from the carelessly exposed campfires of the soldiers there.

That particular outfit now under the threat of the mortar battery always stayed in the same bivouac site when patrolling in the area. The brush had long before been cleared away, and such conveniences as latrines and fire pits had already been dug. It was a very comfortable place to hole up and goof off.

This was an ARVN (Army of the Republic of Vietnam) unit full of draftees and second-rate NCOs and officers. Close to useless, they had been assigned to what was considered a quiet sector of the war.

It was not to remain that way long.

The commander again turned his head to face his mortar crews. They still wore the tan uniforms they had brought from home. He reminded himself to make a stronger extra effort to get them clothing more suitable for jungle terrain. Their garments had been designed for a mountainous dry climate. Such discomfort was only another test of their devotion to duty.

The officer felt proud of his men as he called out to them loudly:

*"Khallas!"*

The assistant gunners slid the fins of the mortar ammo inside the tubes. They waited in happy anticipation for the next command. It wasn't long in coming.

*"Atlak!"*

During the next few moments, a half dozen rounds were dropped into the waiting barrels. That made a grand total of twenty-four that followed the correct trajectory to drop into the South Vietnamese army camp.

Within fifteen seconds of the command to fire, explosions erupted from the woods. Pieces of trees, equipment and men were belched high into the air by the efficient, killing barrage.

Then an eerie silence filled the scene. Even the mortarmen sensed the macabre atmosphere, and they stood without speaking by their weapons. The somber moment was broken by the commander. He tilted his head back and laughed, calling out in a shrill voice:

*"Jezayirli riji Indochine!* The Algerians have returned to Indochina!"

# Chapter 1

The B-Team Camp called Nui Dep was located in west central South Vietnam on the Cambodian border. Although rather stark and spartan by the usual standards of Western civilization, this fortified hamlet was the proverbial lap of luxury when compared with the six A-Team Camps it supported. It could also boast of an airstrip capable of supporting C-130 transport aircraft, and a large helicopter pad for that phase of aerial activity. All this was directed from a "control tower" which was no more than a bunker located to one side of the airfield. The establishment of this type of structure was through necessity not choice. The little post was under frequent attack by Viet Cong light and heavy weapons. A tall structure would not have lasted twenty-four hours.

Normally Nui Dep was the home of the host B-Team and local militia along with some occasional itinerant units billeted there on a temporary basis for specific missions. It got crowded at times and the commanding officer and his men would get a bit grumpy and mumble to themselves about the inconsideration of the brass in Saigon for foisting those squatters on them, but things would get back to normal after a time and the camp's permanent population could once again stretch out and get back to their deadly business of counterinsurgency in the surrounding countryside.

Then the unwelcomed report arrived.

The commander, a dour major named Riley, received the message just after evening chow. It was early evening before dark—the most peaceful time of day at Camp Nui Dep—and Riley had stuffed himself with some of the roast pork the indigenous kitchen crew had prepared. He sat in his hootch contemplating life between sips of Budweiser and draws on a two-for-a-dime stogie when the commo sergeant pounded on his door frame.

"Bad news, sir."

Riley sat the beer down and stepped outside. "What's going on? Did the North Vietnamese launch a major offensive?"

"Worse than that, sir," the sergeant said. "Falconi and his boys are coming back."

The major's face blanched in anger. Then he calmed down and shrugged in the philosophical way of soldiers used to hardship, inconvenience and happy-horseshit situations. "Hell! We can stand 'em for a few weeks without going bananas, can't we?"

The sergeant's face remained somber. "Sir—the bastards are coming to stay."

"To stay? What the hell do you mean *to stay*?"

"Nui Dep is gonna be their permanent headquarters 'til further notice, Major."

"Oh, shit!"


Maj. Robert Falconi stared out the door of the vibrating H34 chopper that was carrying him and his detachment out to Nui Dep. There were six men inside the aircraft with him, not counting the pilot. Since all had their bag-and-baggage, the compartment was a trifle crowded.

14

Falconi thought about lighting up a cigarette, but the prop blast whipping in through the wide opening of the doorway would have made that difficult to do. He glanced around the interior of the chopper and studied the faces of the men with him.

Master Sgt. Duncan Gordon, the Black Eagles Detachment operations sergeant and top kick, dozed with the nonchalance of the seasoned trooper he was. He'd come into their unit from the spit-and-polish cloistered world of the Eighty-second Airborne Division, and he'd had to turn 180 degrees out on his personal opinions of what soldiering was. But he'd ended up being a damned fine senior NCO for such a wild-assed unit.

There was no napping for Sfc. Ray Swift Elk. This full-blooded Sioux from South Dakota was a direct descendant of the warriors who held the United States Army at bay over a long period of years in the nineteenth century. Dark complected, with a hawk nose — and keen, darting eyes to match — this man went to war like it was what he'd been born for.

Perhaps, Falconi mused, that's why he's probably the best adjusted individual he'd ever met in the Army.

The detachment's heavy weapons leader, a muscular South Korean marine master sergeant named Chun Kim, slept soundly off in one corner. He'd suffered a serious wound in which most of the deltoid muscle on his right shoulder had been blown away, but stubborn perseverance and incredible physical control developed through years of study as a *karateka* had brought him through the ordeal to a splendid recovery. He snoozed peacefully, with both arms wrapped tightly around his pet — an M79 grenade launcher.

Falconi grinned at the sight, then swung his gaze to the next man.

Calvin Culpepper, a young black off a sharecropper's

15

farm in Georgia, handled the detachment's explosive chores. This veteran sergeant first class was reputed to be able to put a shaped charge under a silver dollar, then touch it off and get back ninety-nine cents in change.

Sfc. Malcomb McCorckel — affectionately called "Malpractice" — was the team medic. As nagging and worrisome as a mother hen, he took his responsibilities serious enough to make himself a real pain in the ass — literally when it came to penicillin shots — but the other members of the detachment tolerated his needling. There had been several times when Malpractice had completely disregarded his own safety to go through heavy enemy fire to retrieve a badly wounded Black Eagle.

The final passenger in the group was the most unusual. No other unit in no other army had a character like Archibald Dobbs the detachment scout. A brawling, beer-drinking womanizer, Archie Dobbs was a one-man public scandal and disaster area in garrison or in town. He'd been up and down the ranks so much that his uniform issue bore the chevrons of all ranks between the grades of private first class and staff sergeant. But the one redeeming talent he had — combined with plenty of physical courage — was an uncanny ability to never lose his way. Like the cat who always landed on his feet, Archie could be dropped into the middle of any geographic hell and find his way out. His sense of direction was flawless, making Archie Dobbs the man-of-the hour on several Black Eagle missions during dangerous exfiltration operations when everything had gone totally to shit.

Falconi turned his eyes to the jungle that crept by a couple of thousand feet below them. Down there, beneath the canopy of trees, was where he and his men did their jobs. It was, in effect, their office or shop in the same way as the working places of accountants and mechanics.

That type of terrain was what was known as a monsoon forest — or, as the more sophisticated called it, a *tropical deciduous forest* — which occurs in areas with tremendous amounts of rainfall but also long dry seasons. The main difference between this vegetation and a rain forest is that there is more light penetration down into the depths. This also results in much more undergrowth which causes interlopers to make unwanted noise while it provides cover for defenders.

Unfortunately for the Black Eagles, their mission always made them the interlopers.

The pitch of the chopper engine changed and the fuselage tipped as the aircraft swung onto the correct azimuth for its approach and landing. Falconi looked down and saw the B-Team Camp at Nui Dep for a brief glance before the helicopter lined up for the run in.

The change in the H34's attitude broke the passengers' lethargy and all sat up as their journey went into its final gyrations. Within moments the tops of trees were visible straight out the door, and dust flew up from the landing pad. When the helicopter's weight bounced on the shocks, Falconi signaled the others to follow as he grabbed up his gear and jumped out onto the hard-packed ground. He continued off the pad toward the three Green Beret types who waited for him.

The H34's engine revved up again as it shot skyward to resume whatever the rest of its mission was. Falconi instinctively shook his head at the quiet that assailed his punished ears after an hour and a half of chopper motor roaring.

Major Riley, his arms folded, greeted the newcomer with a scowl. "Howdy, Falconi."

"Howdy, Riley." Falconi grinned. "We're back."

17

"Any reports or messages to deliver from higher headquarters?"

"Nary a one," Falconi said.

"OK. Now that proper military protocol has been satisfied and I've greeted you, I'll turn you over to my S-4 sergeant."

"It was nice seeing you again, Riley."

"Fuck you very much, Falconi." The officer turned abruptly and strode back to his hootch.

"Thank you, Riley, and we're happy to be back here too!" Falconi called after the departing Green Beret commander.

The supply sergeant displayed as much happy enthusiasm as had his commanding officer. "This way, sir."

"You sticking us back in that same old bunker?" Falconi asked.

"Yes, sir. We moved the supplies out yesterday," the sergeant said.

Top Gordon, following behind with the rest of the Black Eagles, tapped the other NCO on the shoulder. "We'll have to have you over once we're settled in."

"I'd be delighted," the sergeant said, "once you jokers have fixed up the latrine, that is."

The bunker was at the edge of the camp. It had originally been built as an auxiliary supply area, but the Black Eagles' first arrival on the scene had caused that to change. Falconi and his men had fixed the place up, then been moved out. Riley then had it reverted to a supply room, but once again Falconi had made an appearance.

The cycle continued several times, until this encore performance. The bunker home of the Black Eagle Detachment was empty, dirty and desolate. Top Gordon stepped inside first and looked around. "Oh, my God!" he moaned. Then he went back outside. "Drop your gear, guys." He motioned to Archie. "See if that chickenshit supply sergeant will let us have some brooms."

"Is it that bad, Top?" Falconi asked.

Gordon nodded. "Yes, sir. But as the old song goes, 'Be it ever so humble, there's no place like home.' "

The Black Eagles were the brainchild of a Central Intelligence Agency case officer named Clayton Andrews.

In those early days of the 1960s, Andrews had been doing his own bit of clandestine fighting which involved more than harassment missions in Viet Cong areas. His main job was the conduct of operations into North Vietnam itself. When this dangerous assignment was expanded, Andrews began an extensive search for an officer to lead a special detachment he needed to carry out certain down-and-dirty missions. After hundreds of investigations and interviews, he settled on a Special Forces captain named Robert Falconi.

Pulling all the strings he had, Andrews saw to it that the Green Beret officer was transferred to his own branch of SOG—the Special Operations Group—to begin work on a brand new project.

Captain Falconi was tasked with organizing a new fighting unit to be known as the Black Eagles. This group's basic policy was to be primitive and simple: Kill or be killed!

Their mission was to penetrate deep into the heartland of the Communists to disrupt, destroy, maim and slay. The men who would belong to the Black Eagles would be volunteers from every branch of the armed forces. And that was to include all nationalities involved in the struggle against the Red invasion of

South Vietnam.

Each man was to be an absolute master in his particular brand of military mayhem. He had to be an expert in not only his own nation's firearms but also those of other countries, friendly and enemy alike. But the required knowledge in weaponry didn't stop at the modern ones. It also included knives, bludgeons, garrotes and even crossbows when the need to deal silent death had arisen.

There was also a requirement for the more sophisticated and peaceful skills, too. Foreign languages, land navigation, communications, medical and even mountaineering and scuba diving were to be within the realm of knowledge of the Black Eagles.

They became the enforcement arm of SOG, drawing the missions which were the most dangerous and sensitive. In essence they were hit men, closely coordinated and completely dedicated, held together and directed through the forceful personality of their leader, Maj. Robert Falconi.

After Clayton Andrews was promoted out of the job, a new CIA officer moved in. This was Chuck Fagin. An ex-paratrooper and veteran of both World War II and the Korean War, Fagin had a natural talent when it came to dreaming up nasty things to do to the unfriendlies up north. It didn't take him long to get Falconi and his boys busy.

Their first efforts had been directed against a pleasure palace in North Vietnam. This bordello par excellence was used by Communist officials during their retreat from the trials and tribulations of administering authority and regulation over their slave populations. There were no excesses, perverted tastes or unusual demands that went unsatisfied in this hidden fleshpot.

Falconi and his wrecking crew skydived into the

perational area in a HALO (High Altitude Low Opening) infiltration, and when the Black Eagles finished their raid on the whorehouse, there was hardly a soul left alive to continue the debauchery.

Their next hell-trek into the enemy's hinterlands was an even more dangerous assignment with the difficulty factor multiplied by the special demands placed on them. The North Vietnamese had set up a special prison camp in which they were perfecting their skills in the torture-interrogation of downed American pilots. With the conflict escalating in Southeast Asia, they rightly predicted they would soon have more than a few Yanks in their hands. A North Korean brainwashing expert had come over from his native country to teach them the fine points of mental torment. He had learned his despicable trade during the Korean War when he had American POWs directly under his control. His use of psychological torture, combined with just the right amount of physical torment, had broken more than one man despite the most spirited resistance. Experts who studied his methods came to the conclusion that only a completely insane prisoner could have resisted the North Korean's methods.

At the time of the Black Eagles' infiltration into North Vietnam, the prisoners behind the barbed wire were few—but important. A U.S.A.F. pilot, an Army Special Forces sergeant and two high-ranking officers of the South Vietnamese forces were the unwilling tenants of the concentration camp.

Falconi and his men were not only tasked to rescue the POWs but also had to bring along the prison's commandant and his North Korean tutor. Falconi pulled the job off, fighting his way south through the North Vietnamese army and air force to a bloody showdown on the Song Bo River. The situation deteriorated to the point that the Black Eagles' magazines had their last few rounds in them as they waited for the NVA's final charge.

The next operation took them to Laos where they were pitted against the fanatical savages of the Pathet Lao. If that wasn't bad enough, their method of entrance into the operational area was bizarre and dangerous. This type of transport into battle hadn't been used in active combat in more than twenty years. It had even been labeled obsolete by the military experts. But this didn't deter the Black Eagles from the idea.

They used a glider to make a silent flight to a secret landing zone. Plus the operations plan called for their extraction through a glider-recovery apparatus that had never been tested in combat.

After a hairy ride in the flimsy craft, they hit the ground to carry out a mission designed to destroy the construction site of a Soviet nuclear power plant the Reds wanted to install in the area. Everything went wrong from the start, and the Black Eagles fought against a horde of insane zealots until their extraction to safety. This was completely dependent on the illegal and unauthorized efforts of a dedicated U.S.A.F. pilot—the same one they had rescued from the North Vietnam prison camp. The Air Force colonel was determined to help the men who had saved him, but many times even the deadliest determination isn't enough.

This episode was followed with a mission that had been doubly dangerous because of an impossibility to make firm operational plans. Unknown Caucasian personnel, posing as U.S. troops, had been committing atrocities against Vietnamese peasants. The situation had gotten far enough out of control that the effectiveness of American efforts in the area had been badly damaged. Once again Falconi and the Black Eagles were called upon to sort things out. They went in on a dark beach from a submarine and began a deadly reconnaissance until they finally made contact with their quarry. These enemy agents, wearing U.S. Army uniforms, were dedicated East German Communists prepared to fight to the death for their cause. The Black Eagles admired such unselfish dedication to the extent that they gave the Reds the opportunity to accomplish that end — give their lives for communism. But this wasn't accomplished without the situation deteriorating to the point the Black Eagles had to endure human wave assaults from a North Vietnamese army battalion led by an infuriated general. This officer had been humiliated by Falconi on the Song Bo River several months previously. The mission ended in another Black Eagle victory — but not before five more men had died.

Brought back to Saigon at last, the seven survivors of the previous operations had cleaned their weapons, drawn fresh, clean uniforms and prepared for a long-awaited period of R&R.

It was not to be.

Chuck Fagin's instincts and organization of agents had ferreted out information that showed a high-ranking intelligence officer of the South Vietnamese army had been leaking information on the Black Eagles to his superiors up in the Communist north. It would have been easy enough to arrest this double agent, but an entire enemy espionage net had been involved. Thus, Falconi and his Black Eagles had to come in from the boondocks and fight the good fight against these spies and assassins in the back streets and alleys of Saigon itself.

When Saigon was relatively cleaned up, the Black Eagles drew a mission that involved going out on the Ho Chi Minh trail on which the North Vietnamese sent supplies, weapons and munitions south to be used by the Viet Cong and elements of the North Vietnamese army. The enemy was enjoying great success despite repeated aerial attacks by the U.S. and South Vietnamese air forces. The high command decided that only a sustained campaign conducted on the ground would put a crimp in the Reds' operation.

Naturally, they chose the Black Eagles for the dirty job.

Falconi and his men waged partisan warfare in its most primitive and violent fashion with raids, ambushes and other forms of jungle fighting. The order of the day was "kill or be killed" as the monsoon forest thundered with reports of numerous types of modern weaponry, while the more insidious and deadly form of mine warfare made each track and trail through the brush a potential zone of death.

When this was wrapped up, Falconi and his troops received an even bigger assignment. This next operation involved working with Chinese mercenaries to secure an entire province ablaze with infiltration and invasion by the North Vietnamese army. This even involved beautiful Andrea Thuy, a lieutenant in the South Vietnamese army who had been attached to the Black Eagles. Playing on the mercenaries superstitions and religions, she became a "Warrior-Sister," leading some of the blazing combat herself.

An affair of honor followed this mission, when Red agents kidnapped this lovely woman. They took her north—but not for long. Falconi and the others pulled a parachute-borne attack and brought her out of the hellhole where her Communist tormentors had put her.

The last mission, pulled off with most of the detachment's veterans away on R&R, involved a full-blown attack by North Vietnamese regulars into the II Corps area—all this while saddled with a pushy newspaper reporter.

During these times, as unit integrity and morale built up, the detachment decided they wanted an insignia all their own. This wasn't at all unusual for units in Vietnam. Local manufacturers, acting on decisions submitted to them by the troops involved, produced these emblems that were worn by the outfits while "in country." These adornments were strictly non-regulation and unauthorized for display outside of Vietnam.

Falconi's men came up with a unique beret badge manufactured as a cloth insignia. A large version was used as a shoulder patch. The design consisted of a black eagle—naturally—with spread wings. Looking to its right, the big bird clutched a sword in one claw and a bolt of lightning in the other. Mounted on a khaki shield that was trimmed in black, the device was an accurate portrayal of its wearers: somber and deadly.

Now, back at their old home at Nui Dep, Falconi and his men settled in to await reinforcements and the arrival of the CIA operative Chuck Fagin to brief them on their newest mission. They didn't know what it was, but whatever the Gods of War had ordained for them, the Black Eagles would follow the Latin motto they had adopted for themselves:

*CALCITRA CLUNIS*—KICK ASS!

# Chapter 2

It took three long days of hard work, but the bunker was finally made into a real home.

The sagging bunk frames were repaired and fastened to the walls; the floorboards were wetted down, swept and dry-mopped back to cleanliness; broken sandbags on the roof and along the sides were replaced, and the firing positions that faced outward were reinforced and brought back to usable conditions.

The final touch was the furniture. Crude but functional, the stools and tables had been laboriously fashioned through the carpentry talents of Calvin Culpepper and Malpractice McCorckel. Old ammo crates, shipping boxes and stray pieces of lumber had been begged and borrowed along with necessary nails and screws. The grumpy camp S-4 sergeant had broken down and magnanimously let them use his own personal hammer and saw for the chore.

That third evening found the Black Eagles staying in to celebrate the end of the chore with some iced down cans of Budweiser. Archie Dobbs chug-a-lugged his first can, then belched loudly as he reached for another. "Back to the war, hey, guys?"

"That's it, baby," Calvin said, slowly assuaging his thirst with gentle sips of beer.

Malpractice sighed. "That R&R was the best I've

ever been on. Too bad it had to end."

"I'll have to take your word for it," Top Gordon said. "Seeing as how the major and I were either packed in plaster or recovering through PT while you jokers were out enjoying yourselves."

Archie, Malpractice and Blue Richards had gone off on their own while Calvin and Kim the Korean marine pursued their interests in various gambling establishments in Hong Kong.

Archie smiled in a contented but melancholy sort of way. "Those three women we met were the finest, best-looking ladies I've ever known."

"They sure as hell were!" Malpractice agreed. He lifted his can of beer. "Here's to 'em, God bless 'em!"

"Real classy dames, huh?" Top Gordon asked.

Blue Richards got a dreamy look in his eyes. "You bet! Julie, Janet and Alda!"

Archie joined the toast. "Do you suppose those gals are married?" he wondered aloud.

"Well, if they are," Blue Richards conceded, "it's to three of the luckiest bastards in the world."

"No one's good enough for 'em," Malpractice said with solemnity.

Major Falconi, who had spent most of his own R&R after getting out of the hospital locked up in the office of Chuck Fagin, could only listen in envy as his men relived their wild days and nights of revelry. "I hate to add a note of seriousness to this happy-assed conversation, but I thought you'd like to know the new men are coming in tomorrow."

Calvin Culpepper finished his beer and crushed the can. "How do they stack up, sir?"

"Yes, Major," Kim said. "Please to tell us of our new friends."

"I personally went over their 201 files and interviewed them," Falconi said. "We've got good, experi-

27

enced people coming in."

Archie was impatient. "What about the next mission, Skipper? You know all about it, right?"

"Wrong. Fagin will be coming out with the replacements," Falconi said. "He'll give us the dope on our next little venture into hell." The major started to elaborate when an angry scuffle of boots sounded outside.

"Falconi!" It was Riley's voice and he wasn't in a good mood.

Falconi stood up. He instinctively eyed Archie Dobbs. "What the hell have you been up to?"

Archie displayed an expression of cherubic innocence. "Who? Me?"

The other Black Eagles, anticipating knuckle drill, removed their fatigue jackets as Falconi went to the door of the bunker and stepped out. He glanced up the earthen steps leading to ground level.

Riley, with three of his senior NCOs, stood there with his hands on his hips. "Enjoying yourself this evening, Falconi?"

Falconi shrugged. "Sure." He walked up to ground level with his men closely following.

Riley smiled sardonically. "Is your beer nice and cold?"

"Yeah."

"Well, Falconi," Riley snarled, "mine *ain't*!"

"I'm right sorry to hear that, fella," Falconi said. "But remember what General Sherman said, 'War is a terrible inconvenience'—or something to that effect."

Riley ignored the poor attempt at humor. "My beer is warm, because one of your pig-fuckers stole our ice."

Falconi shot a glance at Archie. The detachment scout's self-conscious grin dispelled any doubts there might have been about his guilt.

Riley continued, "That fucking ice machine only

28

works for a while during the day. It draws a lotta juice
off the generator, so we can't just make ourselves tons
of ice. Naturally, we don't appreciate it when you or
your pig-fuckers steal what we've made for our own
use."

"I'm not saying we didn't do it, and I'm not saying we
did," Falconi said. "But none of my guys are pig-
fuckers, Riley."

"Oh, they ain't?"

"Nope. I can personally guarantee that none of 'em
have been anywhere near your sister," Falconi said
pleasantly.

"Not today, anyhow," Archie added.

Riley's fist whistled through empty air as Falconi
ducked under the straight right and came up with a left
uppercut that connected solidly under the other major's
chin.

Riley flipped back like he'd been hit by a jeep.

Archie let out a yell and brushed past Falconi to
charge straight into the burly camp supply sergeant.
The NCO took the attack straight into his big chest.
After Archie bounced back, the man slammed a big fist
straight into the scout's face. Archie, his eyes rolling,
was already out cold as he backpedaled back into Top,
Malpractice, Kim, Blue and Swift Elk with such force
that all six tumbled down the dugout steps.

The sergeant spun on his heel and aimed a round-
house right at Falconi's head. The major made a *jodan
uke* block, then responded with a combination of rights
and lefts that snapped the NCO's head back and forth.
To the man's credit, he managed to swing punches
twice more before he dropped from a left jab that was
straight into the nose. Falconi felt the breathing organ
give way under the punch and saw large specks of
blood splatter out.

But Riley was back in action. Unfortunately for

him, Swift Elk, Kim, Blue and Malpractice had untangled themselves from their unconscious pal Archie They collided with the major as they leaped out of the dirt stairway. All went down, while Riley's other two NCOs joined the fray.

Falconi didn't wait for an invitation, he just jumped in. More of Riley's men, who had been at their own hootches nearby, rushed over to join the fight. The brawl disintegrated into a mass of cursing, punching, snarling Special Forces and Black Eagle men:

"Take that!"

"Sonofabitch — you godamned sonofabitch!"

"Ow! Who bit me?"

"Dirty bastard! Hey, it's me, Kim!"

"Oh! Sorry, Top!"

"Fucking Falconi, I'm gonna pulverize your ass!"

The mini-riot was joined by even more of the camp's men. The additional combatants added to the noisy spectacle.

The local native militia, attracted by the noise, gathered around laughing and pointing at their American companions. Their women and little children squealed and laughed with delight as the blood flew and dust rose in the fading twilight.

Then the shit really hit the fan.

The first three mortar shells fell onto the outer wire, sending up roaring geysers of dirt.

"Incoming rounds!"

The brawlers quickly untangled themselves and limped off to their combat stations as another trio of explosions rocked the area.

Kim was the first Black Eagle down the steps. The Korean marine grabbed Archie, who was just sitting up with a blank expression on his face, and dragged him inside.

The others stumbled in, grabbing helmets and M16

30

rifles, before rushing straight to their firing positions. By then the barrage was going strong. The earth rocked with each booming explosion, and the bunker's roof shook, sending down fine clouds of dust and other debris.

Archie shook his head, trying to clear the cobwebs of lingering unconsciousness from his brain. "Jeez, I'm gonna have a headache!" he complained loudly.

Top Gordon, his jaw aching, growled. He pushed his mouth up to Archie's ear and hollered, "The next time you steal something, try to show a little class—like don't get caught!"

Archie could barely hear the detachment's top kick. He leaned toward him and yelled, "I couldn't take time to be cute, Top. The fucking ice was melting!"

Before the two could engage in any more of the difficult conversation, Falconi and the others' M16s barked. Archie and Top rushed to their firing parapets.

The mortar fire was slowly lifting as flares were fired up by the defenders. The eerie white light cast by the illumination devices showed the Viet Cong attackers moving through the ruined wire toward the camp's outer defenses.

More M16 fire, augmented by several well-placed M60 machine guns, raked through the attackers. The front rows of the Reds melted under the steel hailstorm, but their comrades bringing up the rear pressed on, passing through the deadly flying bullets by the advantage of the sheer weight of numbers.

Kim, excited, got his M79 grenade launcher and shoved a forty-millimeter round into the barrel. He snapped it back in place for action, then began a routine he was famous for in the Black Eagles—a steady, syncopated rate of single-shot fire.

The small explosions burst out in the front rank, going irregularly from right to left to right to center, twice to the right, etc., causing the attackers to slow and hesitate in the unpredictable incoming fire.

But more of them stacked up behind the fallen, then pressed on closer to the bunker.

It seemed the field of fire in front of the Black Eagles was filling up with little bastards in pith helmets and black pajama uniforms. Malpractice and Calvin were on full automatic now, sweeping the area with overlapping bursts of 5.56-millimeter rounds. Falconi, Swift Elk and Archie continued with hasty, but well-aimed semi-automatic firing.

And Kim continued his mini-artillery barrages with the M79, but the VC attack pressed in closer despite the bodies that were piling up in front of the bunker.

Then the grenade bounced through the firing slit.

Archie Dobbs' mind dully identified it as a Chinese Communist Type F1 as he dived for it. He grabbed the hissing fragmentation instrument and rolled over to throw it at the narrow opening.

Ray Swift Elk ducked as the grenade zipped past him and bounced onto the dirt outside. He was joined on the floor by the other Black Eagles as the thing detonated and sprayed out hunks of metal for twenty meters.

There was no time for congratulations. The Black Eagles leaped back to their firing positions and renewed their efforts to blow away the sons of bitches pressing in on them.

After another long quarter of an hour, the battle began a slow subsidence. The Viet Cong broke contact and withdrew in a measured, disciplined pace back across the wire while a covering barrage of more mortar fire slammed into the camp.

Suddenly it was over.

The camp's Special Forces men quickly moved out into the darkness in pursuit as far as practical—which wasn't a great distance under the circumstances — then returned. They had found that all the enemy dead and wounded had been withdrawn by the retreating Viet Cong.

Ray Swift Elk shook his head and glanced at Archie. "What the hell were you trying to do? Hit me with that fucking grenade?"

"Aw, hell!" Archie said in false modesty, "I would've just held it in my hands, but I was afraid some of the shrapnel might get through my fingers and hurt you guys."

Top Gordon, ever the first sergeant, checked his men. "You guys OK?"

They answered in the affirmative. Falconi motioned to them. "Let's get out of here and up into the fresh air."

They needed no urging, and quickly scrambled up the steps after their commander. A glance at the defensive area showed the damaged wire and dark spots on the ground where pools of blood had collected. But no enemy casualties.

"What the hell did the little fuckers gain by all this?" Malpractice asked.

Swift Elk lit a cigarette. "They're just letting us know they own the land out there at night."

"Yeah," Falconi agreed. "Even if we chased 'em deep into the jungle, they'd have ambushes set up to waylay us."

"I don't like being hemmed in like this after dark," Archie complained. "I hope the mission coming up gets us out and moving."

"Hardcore, ain't you?" Calvin Culpepper said grinning.

Further conversation was interrupted by the arrival of Major Riley and a couple of his men. The commander's right eye was discolored and swollen shut. He looked at Falconi with the good left one. "Any casualties?"

"None here," Falconi said.

"Good. We took a couple," Riley said wearily. "One'll make it, the other won't."

"Need any help?" Malpractice the medic asked.

"No, thanks," Riley said. "If we do, I'll send somebody for you."

"Yes, sir."

Falconi slung his M16 over his shoulder. "You and your guys there want a beer?"

Riley grinned. "Is it cold?"

"Sure. C'mon." Falconi led him down into the bunker. He looked back at his fellow major. "I'm sorry about that crack about pig-fuckers and your sister. You had a right to get pissed off and take a swing at me."

Riley laughed loudly. "Hell, Falconi! I don't even have a sister!"

The group of men who had been pounding the daylights out of each other a scant hour and a half previously now sat quietly drinking Budweiser together.

The brawl between the Americans had been the "Pier Six" variety, yet not one man had thrown a deadly or crippling karate punch. The only martial art techniques used were blocking movements. All blows struck were standard boxing types according to the Marquis of Queensbury rules. But no one mentioned it during the beer drinking.

They didn't have to.

# Chapter 3

Maj. Omar Ahmar dumped the packet of powdered red wine into the canteen cup. He slowly added cold water, swishing it around to make the mixture as complete as possible. No matter how careful he was, there were always reddish lumps left floating on the surface of the drink.

He took a sip and winced. The stuff tasted terrible. It was out of surplus French army field rations left in Oran after Algeria's independence. Even those hated Europeans didn't want to tote the loathsome stuff back to France with them. Ahmar most certainly wasn't fond of the stuff either, but he had a deep personal reason to consume even this weak alcoholic drink: it was against the Islamic religion to consume intoxicants, and this was his own personal statement of defiance toward an institution he thought kept his people out of the twentieth century.

The food in the rations wasn't much to brag about either. There were some crackers, cheese and a pâté of some unidentifiable meat. But Ahmar had to eat exactly what his men did. And these Algerian Arabs needed lots of training and experience before they could live off the land or consume the food of Vietnam.

Ahmar had begun life as the son of a humble farmworker in the vineyards of French Algeria. His father, a devout Moslem, was a laborer for *Monsieur* LeRoux, the farmer. The gnarled old man bent over and tended the vines, picked the grapes and boxed them up for shipment to the cities. Leroux, hawk-nosed and cheap as hell, supervised this demeaning work with all the haughty snobbishness of the colonial aristocrat that he was.

The Ahmar family — husband, wife and five children — lived in a cramped, stone hovel that boasted two rooms and a kitchen. Their luck was bad, their environment tough and their economic situation could only be described as pure, unadulterated poverty. The family, like the others employed on the Leroux farm, took this with the stoic acceptance of good Moslems. Comforting themselves with the old expression: *Allah wills it*.

But young Omar Ahmar was not of a religious nature. In fact, he was downright resentful of his place in life. And he put the full blame of the intolerable situation on the French. If those European *banduk* would get the hell out of North Africa then he and the other Arabs could live with their own customs, taking it easy and contemplating life over cups of thick, hot *kahwi* between sessions of leisurely work and dominating their women.

Even as a little boy, he would daydream about getting up one day to find that the mighty Allah had snapped his fingers and — poof! — the French had simply disappeared. Then his father could pick the grapes, sell them and keep all the money for himself. They would even move into the Leroux's big house, and have plenty of room.

But Omar was a realist and he didn't believe in this invisible Allah everyone had so much faith in. He knew the French weren't going anywhere, and he also knew that he wasn't about to spend his life like his father's —

in grinding, monotonous, difficult work. So, at the age of eighteen, he joined the army.

A smooth-talking sergeant at the *Bureau de Recruitment* convinced him that the soldier's life was one of glory, good times, excellent pay and fancy uniforms. Ahmar eagerly presented his birth certificate and the official *Certificat de la Police* stating he had not committed any real serious crimes, then took a physical examination. The lad was found hale and hearty, and the sergeant courteously invited him to sign on the dotted line for five years of service in the colonial army of the great French republic.

Ahmar and the other Arab recruits went through a sketchy four weeks of basic training. Afterward, instead of being assigned to a crack *Tirailleur* unit, the young Algerian Arab was posted to a pioneer unit as a *soldat de genie*—in reality, a laborer. He was never issued a rifle—though there was one in the company supply room in his name that he was required to clean weekly—but the one thing he most certainly made plenty use of were hand tools. Ahmar quickly found that, instead of laboring under the stern gaze of Old Man Leroux, he now labored under the sterner gaze of his platoon sergeant.

The pay was shitty, the clothing issue sketchy and second-hand, and there was damn sure little leisure time in the road-building and road-mending world of the pioneers. Ahmar and his buddies dug holes, smashed rocks and rolled boulders as they hacked and hewed roads in areas as diverse as the blistering Sahara and the bone-freezing chill of the Aures Mountains.

But relief finally came.

This was in the early 1950s, and the French were deeply committed to their war in Indochina. A Communist insurgency was threatening to begin toppling the empire, and this call to arms was answered mostly by the paras and the Foreign Legion. It was a nasty guerrilla war in remote areas—areas that needed expert road-builders. Thus, one day, instead of falling out with their picks and shovels, the Algerian pioneers loaded onto trucks for a monotonous journey to the docks of Oran.

There were several long days of confused waiting. At least a dozen times the battalion was mustered with bag-and-baggage only to be told to return to their miserable billets located in an empty government warehouse on the docks. Once they even prepared to get back on trucks to return to their original duties, but this was changed too.

Finally, they were marched up the gangplank of a rusting, lumbering old freighter that had been leased for the transport of troops. This was their home for two weeks of a slow voyage that ended at Haiphong. The seasick, miserable Algerians marched back down a gangplank into the steamy, wet heat of Indochina.

This time there was no hesitation in their duty deployment. The pioneers were sent out into the combat zone where they renewed their roadwork tasks. But this time there was no building, only mending.

The paras and legionnaires caught hell out in the deep jungle. Their convoys were ambushed and mined, leaving messes for the Algerians to clean up. Another odious task was added to their workload. Before filling in holes and clearing the roadblocks away, Ahmar and his buddies first had to clear away the bodies—or hunks thereof—of both French and their enemy, the Viet Minh. This work sickened them at first, then their hearts hardened and their stomachs grew strong enough that they were even able to take chow breaks among the cadavers. Then, with food digesting in their stomachs, they casually resumed throwing the French dead up on trucks or burying the

Viet Minh bodies.

It wasn't long before the Algerian pioneers themselves contributed to the growing casualty lists. Snipers and sneak attacks hit them hard. Lightly armed with French MAS36 bolt-action rifles, they fought back in the frustrating little battles that seemed to explode in their faces, then quickly end with the same suddenness. There was always a pioneer or two dead with a couple biting their lips to keep from displaying the pain they felt from wounds.

Ahmar hated the life and felt little enthusiasm for the war. He fought out of a personal hatred for the little bastards that were killing and maiming his pals, but really didn't give a damn if the Viet Minh won their independence or not.

Early one evening, nearly eight months into their stay in Indochina, the pioneers had just finished filling in two large holes in a road caused by a mine. They'd first pulled the pulpy bodies of dead colonial paras out of the tangled mass of trucks caught in the explosion. Then the pioneers had to wait while engineers arrived to use large wreckers to move the useless vehicles off the road. Then they'd begun their work.

By that time they were damned good at it. The hole was filled with earth and rocks, then tamped and watered down in less than two hours. The Algerians had just situated themselves to enjoy an evening meal and wait for their own trucks to retrieve them.

But it was to be almost a year before they would once again enter a French army camp.

The Viet Minh, unexpected as always, suddenly appeared in the growing darkness. Slugs from looted MAT49 submachine guns and semi-automatic M49 rifles raked the pioneers. They made a valiant stand, but were overwhelmed. With all the officers down, a chief corporal took command and promptly surrendered himself and the forty survivors.

Thus, Omar Ahmar marched off into captivity.

He fully expected to be shot. And at times during the long march through the jungle to the prison camp, he actually hoped he would be. With their hands tied tightly behind them, and given only scant swallows of water, the North Africans stumbled along as they were pushed deeper into the grasping, boiling jungle that closed in on them like a large, smothering green blanket.

Finally, relief came when Omar and his fellow laborer-soldiers were shoved behind barbed wire. They passed the first night under the guns of their guards, then that very next day their carefully orchestrated re-education began.

Their teacher was a mild-looking man with spectacles. He wore the black pajamas and sandals of the Viet Minh, but there was no doubt that he was an educated man — an intellectual in Ahmar's eyes. His name was Ngyun Lim and he launched into his program without hesitation. He knew how to talk to Algerians — especially to young fellows like Ahmar — and he told of how he and his fellow Communists were throwing off the colonial yoke of the French.

Ahmar could certainly relate to that. Whenever he heard the word "colonial," he thought of *Monsieur* Leroux, his father's mean and miserly employer back home. Ahmar began to think that, despite their differences, there were fellows in Indochina who also had their own Leroux to contend with. Thus, it wasn't long before he was able to identify solidly with Ngyun.

He began to ask questions. Ngyun noticed him right away, and — like the actor he was — played to that eager youngster with all the brash gestures and oratory he could muster. Ahmar was taken out of the compound and given special lessons. He was soon joined by a few others, though the majority of the Algerians preferred to sit out their captivity and await whatever fate Allah had in store for them.

Within six months, Ahmar was giving lectures and attempting to rally more of his fellow Arabs to the Communist cause. He managed to persuade a few, though most just liked the idea of more and better rations, and he began to develop a feeling of power. Ahmar liked that. He turned in a couple of dissenters, but Ngyun told him not to do anything that would cause the French to punish or mistrust him after repatriation. In fact, the Viet Minh asked him a big favor: They wanted Ahmar to return to the main compound and become "one of the boys" again. He was to avoid attracting any more attention to himself.

Ahmar was disappointed and hurt until it was explained to him that the Communist movement was truly an international one, and that there were Reds in native Algeria who would take him into their fold when he returned home. Flattered now, and extremely pleased, Ahmar agreed.

He returned to the main prison camp population to patiently sweat out the rest of his time in captivity. Ahmar's enthusiasm for the Communist cause was gradually forgotten by his fellow prisoners, and he accomplished what he was supposed to do—melt into obscurity behind the wire.

There was plenty of action in Indochina during that time, and it finally ended with the Battle of Dien-Bien-Phu. The French there took a hell of a kick in the face, and it was the proverbial beginning of the end.

Negotiations began that finally created North and South Vietnam. Prisoner release was arranged, and Omar Ahmar was marched to almost the exact place he was captured. There he was turned back to the French. After a month of debriefing and the general bullshit routine every army has, Ahmar once again got on an old freighter and headed back for Algeria.

He was paid off, given an honorable discharge and a train ticket home. The money he kept, the discharge paper he threw away and the ticket he sold. Then he stayed in Oran, going to an address given him in Indochina.

The place was a small, smoky Arab cafe deep in the native quarter. Ahmar spoke the proper code words to the owner. After being served a meal, he was told to wait. Within an hour a young Algerian arrived and greeted him by name. There was a brief conversation, then Ahmar was invited to accompany his new friend to another location.

They walked through the narrow, winding streets and alleys until Ahmar was completely baffled and disoriented as to their location. Then he was taken through a gateway that opened onto a large courtyard. Several armed men were there. The largest gave him a rough but thorough search, then led him to a nearby door.

Ahmar was surprised that, instead of an out-and-out Communist organization, he was to work in one that nevertheless demanded that he commit himself unto death: the *Front de Liberation Nationale*, to be known throughout the world as the FLN. His new comrades welcomed him as a fellow traveler, having good use for his military training and expertise — provided he would be agreeable to having those skills honed and led off to another direction.

Ahmar did not hesitate to go along with this new program. But before he became an active participant, Ahmar went through a thorough screening process that even included fingerprints. The FLN wanted to make sure that no agent had taken his identity in order to become a "mole" and burrow deep into their organization. Later, as Ahmar recalled this process, he would laugh, knowing that it was actually more painstaking than his enlistment in the French army.

It was the beginning of an eight-year sojourn into the hell of revolution. Omar Ahmar first went to a hidden training camp where he received combat instruction in the particularly brutal style of fighting called for in guerrilla warfare. Then he was assigned to an active unit that fought long and hard in those same Aures Mountains where he'd frozen and labored building roads. Now he not only pulled ambushes on French paras and legionnaires on those roads, but he blew holes in them that others would now have to repair.

The war peaked with DeGaulle giving in to the FLN's demand for liberation. There was an army revolt, of course. The French officers who had fought with dedication in both Algeria and Indochina felt they had again been deceived into a meaningless defeat. They formed a group called the OAS — *Organization Armee Secrete* — employing the type of warfare in which plastic bombs, massacres and atrocities abounded in plenty. But the end seemed inevitable, and Algeria was finally an independent nation.

Capt. Omar Ahmar was in Tunis at that particular time. The unit he commanded had been given a severe drubbing by elements of the First Foreign Parachute Regiment, and they were licking their wounds. All recovered sufficiently to march gloriously back into Algeria in time for the big parades.

Omar Ahmar decided to leave the army and get into active politicking with the Algerian Communist party. He found he liked the yelling and squabbling of this new life. He worked so hard that he became a minor secretary on a full-time basis. He settled into the routine so completely that he even began to put on

43

weight. But that came to an end when special orders arrived for him. Astounded, he was assigned to a clandestine Red military organization with the rank of major, and assigned to a secret mission.

Within weeks, Omar Ahmar was back deep in the green hell of Indochina.

# Chapter 4

Maj. Robert Falconi and Master Sgt. Top Gordon stood off the helicopter landing pad and watched the H34 chopper ease in for a landing.

The moment the wheels touched down, the pilot killed the engine. Falconi and Top walked forward as several men leaped from the aircraft to the ground. The first one out, a lanky, hard-muscled young man with a short crop of blond hair, waved to the major. "How's it going, sir?"

"Fine, Chris," Falconi said, greeting the man he had chosen to be his second-in-command.

Lt. Chris Hawkins, United States Navy Seals, swung his rucksack up on his shoulder, then grabbed his seabag and hurried off the pad. He was quickly followed by three other men.

The first was also a Navy Seal. This was Chief Petty Officer Leland Brewster, a communications specialist. An older man, he really looked the part of the salty tar. His brawny arms were covered with tattoos, and he walked with the rolling gait of a seafaring man.

The second arrival was obviously an Australian. Sporting a digger hat with its brim turned up on one side, and three downward-pointing chevrons surmounted by a crown sewn onto his sleeves, Staff Sgt. Bill Taylor stepped down from the pad and dropped his gear. He snapped to attention and gave Falconi a sharp salute. "G'day, sir!"

"Nice to see you again, Sergeant Taylor," Falconi said.

The third, and final, passenger was a muscular Marine sergeant. His black hair was nearly shaved to the scalp, and his appearance was that of a man who was a physical-fitness fanatic. Sgt. Jacob Bernstein's right bicep bulged noticeably as he saluted Falconi. He grinned easily. "Sir, the Marines have landed." He looked around, his smile increasing. "Well, hell! At least one of us has."

"Welcome to the Black Eagles," Falconi said. "If it's any consolation to you, there's a Korean marine here too."

Top Gordon, who had already met the men, shook hands. He looked around. "There's somebody missing."

"Right," Chris Hawkins said. "Sergeant Valverde will be arriving shortly."

Top frowned. "What the hell's going on."

Chief Leland Brewster laughed. "That's one Army guy who does things his way."

Top started to growl a reply, but the heavy noise of a big chopper came from a distance. All hands turned toward the sound. Within a couple of minutes, a huge H47A Chinook came in low over the trees. It swung gracefully, but a bit ungainly and came in for a heavy landing. It dwarfed the H34 that sat beside it.

A short, husky Chicano staff sergeant disembarked and trotted over to the group. "Hiya Major," he said cheerfully. Then he motioned to the others. "Can you guys give me a hand?"

Top, his first sergeant's mannerisms surfacing, stepped forward. "What the hell you got going on,

46

Valverde?"

Staff Sgt. Enrique Valverde seemed puzzled at the hostility. "I need some help unloading our stuff, Sarge. I can't lug all that shit off all by myself."

"What *shit*?" Top demanded.

"Our furniture, the refrigerator, generator and all that other stuff," Valverde said. He looked around. "We could use some more guys."

Falconi went up to the big chopper and looked inside. The interior was filled with boxes and crates. A brand new refrigerator, gleaming and bright, sat in the middle of the cargo. He laughed. "Well, Valverde, I'm certainly glad you got it in avocado. It matches our bunker's decor."

Valverde's expression was serious. "Don't say that just to be nice, Major. I can get an offwhite or even burnt sienna if you want it." He pointed to some mattresses. "Those go with the hospital beds in the crates, sir. I figgered the guys would like 'em better'n regular bunks."

"A refrigerator! Hospital beds!" Falconi exclaimed. "Jesus Christ, Valverde! You're a fucking genius."

Valverde was modest. "You hired me to be a supply sergeant, right, sir?"

"That I did."

"Then I'm doing my job."

Top, who had run back to the bunker, reappeared with Ray Swift Elk, Kim, Calvin, Blue, Malpractice and Dobbs. "Let's get that shit off the chopper, guys."

As the men unloaded the goodies that Valverde had brought in with him, Chris Hawkins took Falconi aside. The Navy lieutenant gave his new commander a cigarette, then lit one for himself. "I'm supposed to tell you that Chuck Fagin will be arriving in a couple of hours. They're not going to waste time committing us."

Falconi wasn't pleased. "I'd hoped we could form up

and work out any kinks with some patrol action around here at Nui Dep."

"It'd be a good idea, sir," Chris agreed. "With half the detachment total strangers to the other half, it would help us develop teamwork."

Falconi took a deep drag of the cigarette and expelled the smoke into the still, steamy air. "We've never been able to do things the right way or the easy way since the first day the Black Eagle Detachment was formed. And I suppose we never will."

"If the jobs were easy, there wouldn't be any sense in having Seals or Green Berets—or Black Eagles either," Chris surmised.

"Did Fagin give you any hints on what we'll be doing?" Falconi asked.

"Not a word," Chris replied.

"That smug bastard is as close-mouthed as a Mafia thug," Falconi said. He heard the whine of a three-quarter-ton truck motor. He turned to see Archie Dobbs backing the vehicle up to the chopper pad. The major frowned. "I'm not in the mood for any more fist fights, Archie. Where the hell did you get that vehicle?"

"It's OK, Skipper," Archie yelled out of the cab. "Riley's supply sergeant loaned it to us."

While the new gear was put into the back of the truck, Staff Sgt. Enrique Valverde said goodbye to the Chinook's crew. The big chopper's rotors churned back to life, lifting the aircraft back into the sky.

Falconi, puzzled, grinned at the Chicano NCO. "How the hell did you manage to get exclusive use of a big-assed Chinook, Hank?"

"I called in a favor, sir," Valverde explained.

"Christ!" Falconi marveled. "It must've been one hell of a debt."

Valverde smiled. "I got lots owed me, Major. And I owe a little here and there, too. Well, I got to get these

48

things moving." He turned to help load the three-quarter-ton for its first trip to the Black Eagle bunker. By the time the fourth and final run was ready to go, another chopper — this one another H34 — came in carrying, besides a couple of Riley's men returning from R&R, a third rider.

It was Chuck Fagin, the CIA case officer, who directed the deadly activities of the Black Eagles for SOG — the Special Operation Group.

Fagin leaped out of the aircraft interior, wasting no time as he trotted over to Falconi and Chris. He carried an attache case with him. "Operations plan," he explained. "Where can we talk?"

"How about here?" Falconi suggested.

"How about some place shadier, say under a beer tree," Fagin countered.

"Riley has a bunker close by that's used as a control tower when necessary," Falconi said. "I'm sure he'll let us use it."

Besides being used to direct air traffic, the bunker was also handy when absolute privacy was necessary. Special problems were discussed within the hallowed confines of the sandbagged structure, as were interrogations where people might be inclined to holler a bit.

Riley let them use the place, but he said he'd be goddamned to hell if he'd fetch any beer for them. But the ever-observant Archie Dobbs, who had been hovering nearby after Valverde's goodies were stashed in the Black Eagles' bunker, got a couple of six-packs to them. "They're pretty warm," he said apologetically. "The refrigerator ain't plugged in yet."

"Refrigerator?" Fagin asked as they went down into the small control tower. "You fuckers have a refrigerator?"

"A long story," Falconi said. He put the beer on the table and passed around three cans.

Fagin, always ready, produced a church key from his pockets and magnanimously opened the beer. "Before you ask, I'll tell you. Andrea Thuy is in the States."

"Thanks," Falconi said. "I admit I was more than a bit curious."

"She's even going to college—for real," Fagin elaborated. "And paperwork is in the mill to give her U.S. citizenship."

Falconi's mind filled with pictures of the beautiful woman he loved, but could not have. "She went through hell," he said as though it would be news to Fagin.

"Yeah." Fagin quickly changed the subject back to the present situation. "We got a real weird situation," he said as a way of opening up his briefing.

"Our situations are always weird," Falconi said flatly. "In fact, most are shitty and dangerous."

"Allow me to correct you," Fagin said. "They are *all* shitty and dangerous."

Chris Hawkins, as Falconi's new assistant, thought it best not to join in the conversation. Normally taciturn anyway, he decided to adopt a wait-and-see attitude. He took a pull of the warm beer, then sat down on a wooden stool in one corner of the small room.

When Falconi did likewise, Fagin knew he was on stage. After a couple of quick swallows, he started talking. "There's a two-company-sized group of Algerians operating along the Cambodian-Vietnamese border. Their presence is an open secret between us and the Reds."

Falconi remembered the encounter with the East Germans during Operation Asian Blitzkrieg. "Are they into some real sneaky, lowdown dirty stuff?"

"No more than usual," Fagin answered. "But there's a lot of attention—on the QT—turned on this situation. The Reds want this struggle against our allies and us to also become an international affair. We have South Koreans, Australians, New Zealanders, Thais, Philippinos and Vietnamese working against them. So they want to counter with a few outside volunteers joining their forces."

"Who're the interlopers?" Falconi asked, interested in his future opponents.

"Algerians," Fagin said. "They're a bunch of hardcore young Arab Commies led by a veteran officer of the FLN. If they prove effective, other nationals will be brought in from behind the Iron Curtain to expand the insurgency against us."

Falconi now understood the full picture. "So we're going out to put our asses on the line to make sure the Reds don't look good in the world press."

Fagin ignored the barbed comment. "The Communists are keeping it a secret because if it fails, they'll have a negative image. But, on the other hand, if they get positive results, it'll be a big-assed propaganda coup for them."

"I like your terminology," Falconi said sarcastically. "*Positive results*, huh. That means they'll kill our people, destroy materiel and make life miserable for a couple of hundred thousand Vietnamese rice farmers."

Fagin wasn't apologetic. "I always look at things with a sort of detached, intellectual manner." He got another beer. "Anyhow, the generals in Saigon want the situation neutralized as quickly as possible — by you and your guys, of course."

"Of course," Falconi said. "Can we expect any special help?"

"Yeah. You'll have re-supply flights when you want 'em, and Medevacs when you need 'em."

Falconi was skeptical. "Just how big a radio do you think we can lug through those boondocks, Fagin? It'll take a powerful station to be able to call in stuff from

51

that far out."

"Don't sweat it," Fagin assured him. "All that can be done on your regular commo gear through an ARVN radio relay station already situated out there." He opened his attache case and pulled out some papers and maps. "Now let's get down to some serious considerations here. I'll give you two guys a look at the OPLAN before it's turned over to the men to be rehashed."

The Black Eagles, veteran and newcomer alike, had worked in a happy frenzy as they remodeled the interior of their bunker.

The racks that held their sleeping gear were ripped out and heaved outside. The broken lumber was joined by the furniture that had been so lovingly fashioned by Malpractice and Calvin. It was tossed out with disdain into the growing junk heap.

Several of Major Riley's men had noticed the commotion and watched in amazement as hospital beds, tables, chairs, a couple of desks, lamps and an avocado-colored refrigerator were carried inside the quarters.

One of the camp's Green Berets sneered at them. "Hey, did you ladies forget your TV set?"

Archie Dobbs, waiting for some help in installing the new generator, sneered back, "It's coming in on the next shipment. If you're a nice guy, you can come over on Sundays and watch *Ed Sullivan*."

"Yeah?" the Green Beret said, suddenly serious. "My favorite program is *Petticoat Junction*."

"Hey!" his buddy said, grabbing his arm. "Don't believe everything that fucking Dobbs says."

"Why not, man? Them fuckers got a 'frigerator, ain't they?"

Dobbs laughed and pointed to their discarded home-made furniture. "You guys can have any of that you want."

"Aw, fuck you," the Green Beret said.

His buddy was pragmatic. "I'm gonna get me one o' them chairs."

Others from the camp showed up, and the junk yard disappeared as the lumber and other stuff was picked up by men who could put it to good use.

By the time Falconi, Chris and Fagin had finished their talk, the Black Eagle bunker was refurnished with all the comforts of home. The generator was chugging away, and the refrigerator—fully stocked with beer—was performing the duties to which it had been delegated.

The major stepped into the interior and gasped at the change. There were two desks, tables and chairs set up for working and dining. The big beds, with camouflaged ponchos for mattress covers, were arranged along two sides of the wall. The only remainders of the old setup were the shelves where the men kept their personal belongings.

Top Gordon grinned in delight. He put an arm around Enrique Valverde's shoulders. "This man is remarkable."

"Thanks, Top," Enrique said modestly. "I try to think of myself as no more than an enterprising entrepreneur—a businessman of sorts, who works in an unusual barter system."

"This man," Top said, repeating himself, "is truly remarkable."

Falconi nodded his head in agreement, but there was no gleam of good humor in his eyes.

Top, Archie and the other old sweats knew him well. They recognized something was up. Calvin Culpepper brought it all out into the open. "What's happenin',

Falcon?"

"Tomorrow," Falconi said. "We go into Isolation."

Calvin nodded. "Oh man! The shit's goin' down, baby, the shit's goin' down!"

# Chapter 5

Among the papers that Chuck Fagin brought with him from Saigon was a set known in the military profession as an OPLAN (Operations Plan).

An OPLAN is a brief concept of how a scheduled operation or mission should be conducted. The particular one that Fagin carried into Camp Nui Dep had been aptly designated as *OPLAN Operation Cambodia Challenge*. This document was written by the staff of a higher headquarters who wanted a specific job carried out. Despite the command level, it was not considered to be "etched in stone." Instead it was a set of guidelines and information supplied to Maj. Robert Falconi and his men to which they could add their own input along with other data to create another, much more authoritative paper that would be called the OPORD (Operation Order).

The OPORD was written along strict guidelines that divided it into five basic paragraphs as follows:

1. SITUATION
    a. Enemy Forces (This was the strength, activity, identification, etc. of the bad guys that Falconi and his men were going to face.)
    b. Friendly Forces (These were the good joes that would be participating — or at least be located

damned close—to them during Operation Cambodia Challenge. This included special notes on support capabilities, coordination, cooperation, etc. As in most of the Black Eagles' missions, this paragraph would be labeled as N/A—Not Applicable—since the detachment would be out in the boonies operating on their own.)

2. MISSION

(A simple statement saying exactly what the Black Eagles were supposed to accomplish.)

3. EXECUTION

a. Concept of the Operation (The "How-It's-Gonna-Be-Done" paragraph which included times, dates, organization, specific duties, etc.)

4. ADMINISTRATION AND LOGISTICS

a. Rations

b. Arms and Ammunition

c. Uniform and Equipment

d. Special (Handling of wounded, prisoners, etc.)

5. COMMAND AND SIGNAL

a. Signal (Equipment, call signs, etc.)

b. Command (The chain of command)

This, naturally, took only a page and gave each individual Black Eagle a damned good idea of what was going on without really getting into detail. The finer points would be brought out in annexes, such as supply annex, intelligence annex, infiltration annex, exfiltration annex. These were devised and written out by the men themselves. Specific individuals, according to their specialties, would be assigned to write these annexes and submit them to Major Falconi for his approval. For example, Sfc. Ray Swift Elk, as the detachment intelligence sergeant, wrote the intelligence annex; the supply sergeant Hank Valverde did the supply annex; Malpractice McCorckel composed the medical annex, etc. It is not surprising, therefore, that besides all the tough-guy qualifications to become a Black Eagle, there was also a requirement to be able to type.

Once all this information was brought together, it was hashed, rehashed, and re-rehashed. Only then was it given the final blessing by the Reverend Major Falconi. Then, and only then, could it finally be considered etched in that proverbial stone. In other words, the OPLAN had become an OPORD.

To make sure each man understood every single paragraph of the OPORD, the detachment held a briefing prior to being committed to the mission. This occurred after all that painstaking brainwork had been worked out and put down on paper. Thus, when the Black Eagles left that bunker to take on Ho Chi Minh's fighters, every man knew not only his own job, but those of all his buddies.

All this feverish activity took place in the bunker during a time period designated as Isolation. This terminology could be taken literally. The Black Eagles, following Special Forces procedures, were isolated away from the rest of Camp Nui Dep. Barbed wire was strung around their area, and Major Riley grudgingly provided armed guards to make sure nobody got in or out without proper authority. During this time the only individuals who came and went with any frequency were Major Falconi and the supply sergeant, Valverde. Both had double duty in administrative red tape.

It took seventy-two hours of hard, almost-ceaseless work before it was time for the briefing. Falconi let the boys leave the bunker for a half hour break to breathe some fresh air up at ground level before he went through the door and ascended the steps. Never one to waste words, Falconi communicated to them with but one word:

"Briefing!"

One by one they returned to the earthen confines of their home. The first in was Master Sgt. Top Gordon, the senior noncommissioned officer of the Black Eagles. His position required several tasks. Besides being tasked with taking the OPLAN and using it to form the basic OPORD for the missions, he was also responsible for maintaining discipline and efficiency within the unit. A husky man, his jet-black hair was thinning perceptibly, looking even more sparse because of the strict GI haircut he wore.

Gordon's entrance into the Black Eagles had been less than satisfactory. After seventeen years spent in the Army's elite spit-and-polish airborne infantry units, he had brought in an attitude that did not fit well with the diverse individuals in Falconi's command. Gordon's zeal to follow Army regulations to the letter had cost him a marriage, but he hadn't let up a bit. To make things worse, he had taken the place of a popular detachment sergeant who was killed in action on the Song Bo River. This noncom, called "Top" by the men, was an old Special Forces man who knew how to handle the type of soldier who volunteered for unconventional units. Gordon's first day in his new assignment brought him into quick conflict with the Black Eagle personnel that soon got so far out of hand that Falconi began to seriously consider relieving the sergeant and seeing to his transfer back to a regular airborne unit.

But during Operation Laos Nightmare, Gordon's bravery under fire earned him the grudging respect of the lower-ranking Black Eagles. Finally, when he fully realized the problems he had created for himself, he changed his methods of leadership. Gordon backed off doing things by the book and found he could still maintain good discipline and efficiency while getting rid of the chicken-shit aspects of Army life. It was most apparent he had been accepted by the men when they bestowed the nickname "Top" on him.

He had truly become the top sergeant then.

The next man to enter the bunker was a short, stocky South Korean marine sergeant named Chun Kim. Kim, a heavy weapons infantry expert and third-degree black belt in Tai Kwan Do karate, had been serving continuously in the military since 1948. His experience ran the gamut from the poorly trained and equipped South Korean armed forces that melted under the Communist onslaught from the north in June of 1950, to the later, highly motivated and superbly disciplined elite marines created in the years after the cease fire.

Kim was followed by Sfc. Calvin Culpepper. This tall, brawny black man had entered the Army off a poor Georgia farm his family worked as sharecroppers. He handled the explosive chores that popped up from time to time. His favorite tool was C4 plastic explosive, but he was a virtuoso with the Claymore mine. He used it to its best advantage as well. Ten years of dedicated service in the United States Army had produced an excellent soldier. Resourceful, intelligent and combatwise, Calvin pulled his weight — and then a bit more — in the dangerous undertakings of the Black Eagles.

The detachment medic, Sfc. Malcomb "Malpractice" McCorckel, came in on Calvin's heels. An inch under six feet in height, Malpractice had been in the Army for twelve years. He had a friendly face and spoke softly as he pursued his duties in seeing after the illnesses and hurts of his buddies. He nagged and needled them to keep that wild bunch healthy. They bitched back at him, but not angrily, because each

Black Eagle appreciated his concern. They all knew that nothing devised by puny man could keep Malpractice from reaching a wounded detachment member and pulling him back to safety.

Sfc. Ray Swift Elk was responsible for the unit's intelligence work. A full-blooded Sioux Indian, he was lean and muscular. His copper-colored skin, prominent nose and high cheekbones gave him the appearance of the classic prairie warrior. Twelve years of service in Special Forces made him particularly well-qualified in his slot. His tribe's history included some vicious combats against the black troopers of the U.S. Cavalry's Ninth and Tenth Regiments of the racially segregated Army of the nineteenth century. The Sioux warriors had nicknamed the black men they fought "Buffalo Soldiers." This was because of their hair which, to the Indians, was like the thick manes on the buffalo. The appellation was a sincere compliment due to these native Americans' veneration of the bison. Ray Swift Elk called Calvin Culpepper "Buffalo Soljer," and he did it with the same respect his ancestors had used during the Plains wars.

The man with the most perilous job in the detachment was Staff Sgt. Archie Dobbs. As point man and scout, he went into dangerous areas first, just to see what—or who—was there. Reputed to be the best compass man in the United States Army, his seven years of service was fraught with stints in the stockade and dozens of "busts" to lower rank. Fond of women and booze, Archie's claim to fame—and the object of genuine respect from the other men—was that he had saved their asses on more than one occasion by guiding them safely through throngs of enemy troops behind the lines.

Archie was followed into the bunker by Petty Officer Blue Richards, a Navy Seal. He was a red-haired

Alabaman with a gawky, good-natured grin common to good ol' country boys. Blue had been named after his "daddy's favorite huntin' dawg." An expert in demolitions either on land or under water—Blue considered himself honored for his father to have given him that dog's name.

The first of the new men, Marine Sgt. Jake Bernstein, walked in. A short and muscular New Yorker, he had been a competitive bodybuilder and weightlifter in civilian life. He still exercised as much as possible, and was in a physical condition that could only be described as utterly fantastic. A light weapons infantryman, he had seen some action with the First Marines at Chu Lai and Da Nang prior to joining up with the Black Eagles.

The unit's supply sergeant, a truly talented and enterprising staff sergeant named Enrique "Hank" Valverde, had been in the Army for ten years. He began his career as a supply clerk, quickly finding ways to cut through Army red tape to get logistical chores taken care of quickly and efficiently. He made the rank of sergeant in the very short time of only two years, finally volunteering for the Green Berets in the late 1950s. Hank Valverde found that Special Forces was the type of unit that offered him the finest opportunity to hone and practice his near-legendary supply expertise.

Staff Sgt. Bill Taylor had transferred into the Black Eagles from the Australian army's Second Battalion, Royal Australian Regiment. A tough professional soldier, Taylor came from his country's wild-and-woolly outback. Born and raised in the boondocks, he was more at home in the wilderness than anywhere else. Although belligerent—his own army record during his early years was similar to Archie Dobbs' series of military jails and busts in rank—he had matured emotionally in his early thirties and was able to contro his wild urges, to a point. Blond, husky and sporting a neatly trimmed moustache, he had made it clear to Major Falconi that he would not give up his "digger" hat for even the proud beret of the Black Eagles.

Taylor was followed into the bunker by U.S. Navy Chief Petty Officer Leland Brewster. Although born and bred in Iowa, he was a seagoing man at heart. The myriad of tattoos covering his arms and body attested to his devotion to being a real "sailorman." The only problem Chief Brewster had was that he always found more action ashore. So he volunteered for the Seals in order to enjoy the best of both worlds. With a seamed leathery face and an easy smile, this veteran of fifteen years in the Navy brought diverse and long experience in communications into the Black Eagles with him. He was a natural choice to be Falconi's commo chief.

The final man to enter the bunker was the brand new second-in-command. He was Lt. Chris Hawkins who, like Chief Brewster and Blue Richards, was a Navy Seal. A graduate of Annapolis, he had five years of service which included plenty of clandestine operations on the coast of North Vietnam. A tall, rangy but muscular New Englander who was descended from seven generations of a family devoted to the sea as ships' owners, masters and navigators, he spent his youth sailing and swimming the waters off his native Massachusetts, which made him even more natural of a sailor than Brewster. His service in the Seals combined that seamanship with tough soldiering skills, making him a natural for the Black Eagles.

The men settled down and turned their attention to the front where Maj. Robert Falconi stood waiting for their attention. After a few moments he spoke. "Our mission on Operation Cambodia Challenge is to seek out a detachment of Algerian volunteers, make contact with the unit and destroy them." Falconi paused and looked pointedly at his bloodthirsty charges. "That, gentlemen, does not mean we won't take prisoners." He gave Archie Dobbs a meaningful glance to make sure the scout understood that last statement. Then he continued. "Top Gordon will cover the execution portion of the OPORD."

Top Gordon went to the front of the room as Falconi sat down. He took his pointer, a swagger stick with the bullet of a fifty-caliber round on one end and the casing on the other, and put the point on a spot on a map of central Cambodia. "This is our OA. It's big, but the dense forestry of the area will keep distances down to a minimum. The infiltration phase will be a HALO entry onto this DZ." Again he used the pointer and all men referred to their individual copies of maps of the operational area. "We will exit a C1-30 from an altitude of thirteen thousand feet for a free-fall of approximately sixty seconds."

"Approximately?" Calvin Culpepper asked. "Could you be a little more specificwise, Top?"

"We won't use stopwatches to determine the time for opening. Everyone will have an altimeter on their reserve. Pull those ripcords at fifteen hundred feet."

"What's the terrain there on the drop zone?" Archie Dobbs asked.

"Yeah!" Blue Richards said. "I hope to hell it ain't another damned ol' rice paddy."

"A meadow of thick grass," Top said giving them the good news. "Now, reveille tomorrow is 0300 hours. That means I don't want any last-minute packing in the morning. You be squared away and ready to go tonight before you sack out. Tomorrow all I want you to have to do is chow down, and be out at the landing strip at 0400 hours to draw chutes. We'll chute up and have rigger and jumpmaster checks immediately. Station time on the aircraft, which I've already mentioned is a C-130, is 0430 and take off is 0445."

Ray Swift Elk was curious about the actual jump procedure. "How're we gonna unass that bird, Top?"

Top grinned. He knew they'd like the answer to that question. "Tailgate, baby!"

There was a cheer. That would mean they would go out the open rear cargo hatch rather than the side doors. For HALO—High Altitude Low Opening, which meant jumps using free-fall parachutes—it made for a better controlled exit.

"Once we're on the ground, then things are simple," Top said. "We start looking for them camel-ridin' sons of bitches and blow 'em away. Questions?"

"Now that we know how we're getting *in* there," Jake Bernstein remarked, "I'd like to know how we're getting *out*."

"Exfiltration will be by chopper from the handiest LZ available at that time," Top said. "Any more questions?"

There were none, so the next speaker stepped up. This was Ray Swift Elk who would give the intelligence portion of the briefing. "The bad guys we're looking for are Algerian volunteers in what is thought to be a two-company organization. Their strength is estimated to be a hundred and fifty or so, complete with supporting mortars."

Calvin Culpepper stood up and quickly counted the Black Eagles in the room. "Eleven, twelve, thirteen. OK. That's thirteen of us against a hundred." He looked up at Swift Elk. "You sure that's fair—for them."

Swift Elk laughed. "We can keep your ammo supply down if that's what worrying you, Buffalo Soljer."

Calvin grinned back. "Never mind."

"Those Algerians are a trial mission in which the

64

Reds are testing the use of international volunteers to fight against us and our allies," Swift Elk said. "If they succeed, things might get hairy. However, if we do 'em in and show that jungle fighting ain't for just anybody, we'll make our own efforts in Southeast Asia go smoother."

"We got a helluva lot on the line here, right?" Blue Richards asked.

"A successful foray on our part could prevent the start of World War III," Swift Elk said. "Now, the terrain is the same ol' shit we've been putting up with. Lots o' undergrowth, so it'll take a long time to go short distances. The same for the Algerians, so the fighting will be contained. Sorry there isn't more info on exactly who those North Africans are, but that's all that G2 has been able to dig up. We don't know nothing about their base camps or supply points." He grinned. "But I'm sure we'll find out in due time. Now, if there ain't any questions, I'll turn the floor over to Hank Valverde for the supply poop."

Valverde, harried and busy as always, had his clipboard with him. "Your individual hand weapons have been OK'd to take in," he announced. "But M16s will be the basic tool for messing up the bad guys. The usual issue of ammo and rations will be jumped in by each individual. Malpractice will be carrying extra medical gear while Calvin and Blue will tote the Claymores."

"What about some C-4 plastic stuff?" Calvin Culpepper asked.

"There won't be any," Valverde said. "All demo work will be antipersonnel boom-boom. Also, Kim and me are going to be the grenadiers, so we'll tote M79s and ammo along with our other stuff."

"How does the resupply look?"

"Not too bad," Valverde answered. He pointed to

several areas on the map. "It looks like we'll be able to get extra goodies dropped in to us even though there won't be any regularly scheduled deliveries. Since we don't know where we'll be on a day-by-day basis, or what we'll be doing, I couldn't set up anything on a schedule." He consulted his clipboard. "Hell, I still got to get the parachutes uncrated, so I'll need a detail for that after the briefing. In the meantime, I'll turn the show over to Chief Brewster for the commo information."

Brewster rolled to the front in his sailor's gait. He displayed a leathery, friendly grin. "Ahoy, shipmates. It looks like we'll be doing lots of talking out there so I've made arrangements with Hank Valverde to set us up right. There'll be four Prick-Sixes — one for each team and our scout, Archie Dobbs. Don't worry about any crystal fuck-ups, I've checked all that out and they're all the same. The call signs will be Falcon for the command element. Alpha will be for the Alpha team and Bravo for the Bravo team. I'll tote a PRC-77 in for the main commo chores."

"Who is the main guy we'll be talking to from the field?" Archie Dobbs asked. As scout, he wanted to know where home base was.

"Right here at Nui Dep," Chief Brewster answered.

Bill Taylor the Aussie stood up. "I say, Chief, I'm familiar with your lot's PRC-77. Are you sure we can reach here from the operational area?"

"Don't worry about any problems with distances. There's a clandestine relay station between us and Nui Dep that can pass on our transmissions into here when we need resupply or anything else. Our main call sign for the PRC-77 will also be Falcon and Nui Dep's, of course, is Slick. The call sign for the relay guys is Abner."

There were no more questions regarding communications, so Malpractice McCorckel stepped into the detachment spotlight. "I'll begin with my usual nagging about water purification tablets, treating scratches and insect bites quickly and carefully, salt tablets and so on. Take all the tablets I give you and come to me with even a slight scratch. All of you know they can become seriously infected out there in a short time."

Jake Bernstein had bigger things on his mind. "Suppose something like an AK47 round or a mortar shell gives us a bit more than a scratch, Malpractice?"

"Those same areas we'll use for resupply will be available for Medevac," Malpractice said. "You'll all be issued the usual first-aid stuff, and I'll have my field surgical kit. I only hope you've been brushing your teeth regularly, because I'm not taking the dental kit with me. I'll be damned if I'm gonna tote that damned thing along with the extra claymores and M79 rounds that Hank Valverde has hung on my ass. If there ain't any more questions, I'll turn the floor back to the skipper."

Falconi looked around the bunker and was pleased with what he saw. There were twelve men sitting in front of him, all in the best of physical condition, well-trained, experienced and damned good at what they did. "There's nothing left to do but say good luck." He held up a piece of paper. "Here's the team breakdowns. See who you'll be running with on Operation Cambodia Challenge. I'd advise you to settle any debts and make any necessary apologies with your teammates. Your ass will depend on them."

He posted the roster as Top Gordon reminded them, "Reveille is at 0300 hours."

After he and Falconi left the bunker, they rushed forward to see how the detachment was organized for — as Calvin "Buffalo Soljer" Culpepper so aptly put it — the "shit that was goin' down."

67

## COMMAND ELEMENT

Maj. Robert Falconi, commander
Staff Sgt. Archie Dobbs, scout
Chief Petty Officer Leland Brewster, communications

## ALPHA FIRE TEAM

Lt. Chris Hawkins, team leader
Master Sgt. Chun Kim, grenadier
Sfc. Ray Swift Elk, rifleman
Sfc. Calvn Culpepper, rifleman/demo
Staff Sget. Bill Taylor, rifleman

## BRAVO FIRE TEAM

Master Sgt. Top Gordon, team leader
Staff Sgt. Hank Valverde, grenadier
Sfc. Malpractice McCorckel, rifleman/medic
Petty Officer 3rd Class Blue Richards, rifleman/demo
Sgt. Jake Bernstein, rifleman

# Chapter 6

Falconi had just finished a cigarette down in the bunker. Camp Nui Dep's proximity to Viet Cong activity made noise- and light-discipline an absolute necessity. Therefore, Major Riley quite rightly forbade displaying the glare of lanterns, flashlights or matches after dark. All smoking had to be done in the hot confines of the bunkers with ponchos over the openings to block out any light leakage.

But drinking coffee outside was alright — provided you didn't clank the canteen cup against something — and Falconi sipped a hot mixture of C-ration brew as he sat atop the bunker looking out into the darkness. In a few hours he and the other Black Eagles would hurl themselves out of a high-flying C-130 over difficult terrain where people who would try to kill them now roamed as the lords and masters of the area.

Falconi took another drink of coffee and spoke the words to himself that he'd said many times since taking command of the detachment: "Nobody said this was going to be easy."

Robert Mikhailovich Falconi was born an Army brat

at Fort Meade, Maryland in the year 1934.

His father, 2nd Lt. Michael Falconi, was the son of Italian immigrants. The parents, Salvatore and Luciana Falconi, had wasted no time in instilling an appreciation of America and the opportunity offered by the nation into their youngest son as they had their other seven children. Mister Falconi even went as far as naming his son Michael rather than the Italian Michele. The boy had been born an American, was going to live as American, so—*per Dio e tutti i santi*—he was going to be named as an American!

Young Michael was certainly no disappointment to his parents or older brothers and sisters. He studied hard in school and excelled. He worked in the family's small shoe repair shop in New York City's Little Italy during the evenings, doing his homework late at night. When he graduated from high school, Michael was eligible for several scholarships to continue his education in college, but even with this help, it would have entailed great sacrifice on the part of his parents. Two older brothers, both working as lawyers, could have helped out a bit, but Michael didn't want to be any more of a burden on his family than was absolutely necessary.

He knew of an alternative. The nation's service academies, West Point and Annapolis, offered free education to qualified young men. Michael, through the local ward boss, received a congressional appointment to take the examinations to attend the United States Military Academy.

He was successful in this endeavor and was appointed to the Corps of Cadets. West Point didn't give a damn about his humble origins. It didn't matter to the Academy whether his parents were poor immigrants or not. West Point also considered Cadet Michael Falconi as socially acceptable as anyone in the

Corps regardless of the fact that his father was a struggling cobbler. All that institution was concerned with was whether he, as an individual, could cut it or not. It was this measuring of a man by no other standards than his own abilities and talents that caused the young plebe to develop a sincere, lifelong love for the United States Army. He finished his career at the school in the upper third of his class, sporting the three chevrons and rockers of a brigade adjutant on his sleeves upon graduation.

Second Lieutenant Falconi was assigned to the Third Infantry Regiment at Fort Meade, Maryland. This unit was a ceremonial outfit that provided details for military funerals at Arlington National Cemetery, the guard for the Tomb of the Unknown Soldier and other official functions in the Washington, D.C. area.

The young shavetail enjoyed the bachelor's life in the nation's capital, and his duties as protocol officer, though not too demanding, were interesting. He was required to be present during social occasions that were official ceremonies of state. He coordinated the affairs and saw to it that all the political bigwigs and other brass attending them had a good time. He was doing exactly those duties at such a function when he met a young Russian Jewish refugee named Miriam Ananova Silberman.

She was a pretty brunette of twenty years of age, who had the most striking eyes Michael Falconi had ever seen. He would always say all throughout his life that it was her eyes that captured his heart. When he met her, she was a member of the League of Jewish Refugees attending a congressional dinner. She and her father, Josef Silberman, had recently fled the Red dictator Stalin's anti-Semitic terrorism in the Soviet Union. Her organization had been lobbying Congress to enact legislation that would permit the American government to take action in saving European and Asian Jewry not only from the savagery of the Communists but also from the Nazis who had only begun their own program of intimidation and harassment of Germany's Jewish population.

When the lieutenant met the refugee beauty at the start of the evening's activities, he fell hopelessly in love. He spent that entire evening as close to her as he could possibly be while ignoring his other duties. A couple of Congressmen who arrived late had to scurry around looking for their tables without aid. Lieutenant Falconi's full attention was on Miriam. He was absolutely determined he would get better acquainted with this beautiful Russian. He begged her to dance with him at every opportunity, was solicitious about seeing to her refreshments and engaged her in conversation, doing his best to be witty and interesting.

He was successful.

Miriam Silberman was fascinated by this tall, dark and most handsome young officer. She was so swept off her feet that she failed to play the usual coquettish little games employed by most women. His infectious smile and happy charm completely captivated the young belle.

The next day Michael began a serious courtship, determined to win her heart and marry the girl.

Josef Silberman was a cantakerous, elderly widower. He opposed the match from the beginning. As a Talmud scholar, he wanted his only daughter to marry a nice Jewish boy. But Miriam took pains to point out to him that this was America—a country that existed in direct opposition to any homogeneous customs. The mixing of nationalities and religions was not that unusual in this part of the world. Josef argued, stormed, forbade and demanded—but all for naught. In the end, so he would not lose the affection of his daughter, he gave his blessing. The couple was married in a non-religious ceremony at the Fort Meade post chapel.

A year later their only child, a son, was born. He was named Robert Mikhailovich.

The boy spent his youth on various Army posts. The only time he lived in a town or civilian neighborhood was during the years his father, by then a colonel, served overseas in the European Theater of Operations in the First Infantry Division—The Big Red One. A family joke developed out of the colonel's service in that particular outfit. Robert would ask his dad, "How come you're serving in the First Division?"

The colonel always answered, "Because I figured if I was going to be one, I might as well be a Big Red One."

It was one of those private jokes that didn't go over too well outside the house.

The boy had a happy childhood. The only problem was his dislike of school. Too many genes of ancient Hebrew warriors and Roman legionnaires had been passed down to him. Robert was a kid who liked action, adventure and plenty of it. The only serious studying he ever did was in the karate classes he took when the family was stationed in Japan. He was accepted in one of that island nation's most prestigious martial arts academies where he excelled while evolving into a serious and skillful *karateka*.

His use of this fighting technique caused one of the ironies in his life. In the early 1950s, his father had been posted as commandant of high school ROTC in San Diego, California. Robert, an indifferent student in that city's Hoover High School, had a run-in with some young Mexican-Americans. One of the Chicanos had never seen such devastation as that which Bobby Falconi dealt out with his hands. But the Latin-American kid hung in there, took his lumps and finally went down from several lightning quick *shuto* chops that slapped consciousness from his enraged mind.

A dozen years later, this same young gang member, named Manuel Rivera, once again met Robert Falconi. The former was a Special Forces sergeant first class and the latter a captain in the same elite outfit. Sfc. Manuel Rivera, a Black Eagle, was killed in action during the raid on the prison camp in North Vietnam in 1964.

When Falconi graduated from high school in 1952, he immediately enlisted in the Army. Although his father had wanted him to opt for West Point, the young man couldn't stand the thought of being stuck in any more classrooms. In fact, he didn't even want to be an officer. During his early days on Army posts he had developed several friendships among career noncommissioned officers. He liked the attitudes of these rough-and-tumble professional soldiers who drank, brawled and fornicated with wild abandon during their off-duty time. The sergeants' devil-may-care attitude seemed much more attractive to young Robert than the heavy responsibilities that seemed to make commissioned officers and their lives so serious and, at times, tedious.

After basic and advanced infantry training, he was shipped straight into the middle of the Korean War where he was assigned to the tough Second Infantry Division.

He participated in two campaigns there. These were designated by the United States Army as: Third Korean Winter and Korean Summer-Fall 1953. Robert Falconi fought, roasted and froze in those turbulent months. His combat experience ranged from holding a hill during massive attacks by crazed Chinese Communist forces, to the deadly cat-and-mouse activities of night patrols in enemy territory.

He returned stateside with a sergeancy, the Combat Infantryman's Badge, the Purple Heart, the Silver Star and the undeniable knowledge that he had been born and bred for just one life—that of a soldier.

His martial ambitions also had expanded. He now desired a commission but didn't want to sink himself into the curriculum of the United States Military Academy. His attitude toward schoolbooks remained the same—to hell with 'em!

At the end of his hitch in 1955, he re-enlisted and applied for Infantry Officers' Candidate School at Fort Benning, Georgia.

Falconi's time in OCS registered another success in his life. He excelled in all phases of the rigorous course. He recognized the need for work in the classrooms and soaked up the lessons through long hours of study while burning the midnight oil of infantry academia in quarters. The field exercises were a piece of cake for this combat veteran, but he was surprised to find out that, even there, the instructors had plenty to teach him.

His only setback occurred during "Fuck Your Buddy Week." That was a phase of the curriculum in which the candidates learned responsibility. Each man's conduct—or misconduct—was passed on to an individual designated as his buddy. If a candidate screwed up he wasn't punished. His buddy was. Thus, for the first time in many of these young men's lives, their personal conduct could bring joy or sorrow to others. Falconi's "buddy" was late to reveille one morning and he drew the demerit.

But this was the only black mark in an otherwise-spotless six months spent at OCS. He came out number one in his class and was offered a regular Army commission. The brand-new second lieutenant happily accepted the honor and set out to begin this

75

new phase of his career in an Army he had learned to love as much as his father did.

His graduation didn't result in an immediate assignment to an active duty unit. Falconi found himself once more in school — but these were not filled with hours poring over books. He attended jump school and earned the silver parachutist badge; next was ranger school where he won the coveted orange-and-black tab; then he was shipped down to Panama for jungle warfare school where he garnered yet one more insignia and qualification.

Following that he suffered another disappointment. Again, his desire to sink himself into a regular unit was thwarted. Because he held a regular Army commission rather than a reserve one like his other classmates, Falconi was returned to Fort Benning to attend the Infantry School. The courses he took were designed to give him some thorough instruction in staff procedures. He came out on top here as well, but there was another thing that happened to him.

His intellectual side finally blossomed.

The theory of military science, rather than complete practical application, began to fascinate him. During his time in combat — and the later Army schooling — he had begun to develop certain theories. With the exposure to Infantry School, he decided to do something about these ideas of his. He wrote several articles for the *Infantry Journal* about these thoughts — particularly on his personal analysis of the proper conduct of jungle and mountain operations involving insurgency and counterinsurgency forces.

The Army was more than a little impressed with this first lieutenant (he had been promoted) and sent him back to Panama to serve on a special committee that would develop and publish U.S. Army policy on small-unit combat in tropical conditions. He honed his skills and tactical expertise during this time.

From there he volunteered for Special Forces — the Green Berets — and was accepted. After completing the officers' course at Fort Bragg, North Carolina, Falconi was finally assigned to a real unit for the first time since his commission. This was the Fifth Special Forces Group in the growing conflict in South Vietnam.

He earned his captaincy while working closely with ARVN units. He even helped to organize village militias to protect hamlets, against the Viet Cong and North Vietnamese. Gradually, his duties expanded until he organized and led several dangerous missions that involved deep penetration into territory controlled by the Communist guerrillas.

It was after a series of these operations that he was linked up with the CIA officer Clayton Andrews. Between their joint efforts the Black Eagles had been brought into existence, and it was here that Maj. Robert Falconi now carried on his war against the Communists.

Now, with the tropical night dark and silent over Camp Nui Dep, Falconi finished his coffee. It was at times like this that the major remembered the men who'd gone out on operations and not come back. There had been thirty of them. In a unit that normally numbered not much more than a dozen men, that meant that the Black Eagles had suffered around 250 percent casualties. Faces and names flowed through his mind as the commander paid private respects to good men who'd made the ultimate sacrifice.

Below him, in the bunker, the detachment had completed all last-minute details. The men, their gear packed and weapons loaded, caught a few Z's before Master Sgt. Top Gordon's reveille. Falconi decided he could do with a bit of rest himself. He walked back down into the depths of their earthen domicile, repeating the familiar phase to himself:

"Nobody said this was going to be easy."

# Chapter 7

The sun was only a dull glow on the horizon as the Black Eagles chuted up for their coming mission, but the weather was already hot and muggy.

The jump equipment they struggled into would not be classified as "state of the art" under the strictest of qualifications. The main parachutes were modified U.S. Air Force B-12 free-fall chutes. The canopies had been altered by parachute riggers who cut and sewed them into "Double L's" by cutting out portions of the canopies to increase steering and forward thrust. Toggles, attached to nylon lines that ran down the front set of risors, offered the jumper the option of turning left by pulling the left one or right by tugs on that toggle. The additions of "D" rings and bellybands to hold the reserve parachutes in place completed the alterations.

However, there was an addition above and beyond these design changes. A long, narrow sleeve, surmounted by a pilot chute, was fitted over the canopy to lessen the opening shock when the ripcord was pulled and the B-12 blossomed into life with a loud *whack* of expanding nylon.

The reserve parachutes—a second chance in the case the main parachute malfunctioned—were standard U.S. Army T-7A's. This was the type employed by all paratroopers in their jumping activities.

The job of getting into this gear was a bit more complicated than civilian sport jumpers back in "the world" had to perform. Besides struggling into the parachutes, the Black Eagles also had to hook on their jungle rucksacks and tie down their M16s which they wore at sling arms, with the muzzles down, over their left shoulders. Along with this, Chief Brewster had also to strap the PRC-77 onto his ass. The radio and its battery added a compact twenty-two pounds to his load. Both Calvin Culpepper and Blue Richards toted Claymore mines, Malpractice had his surgical kit, and M79s and grenades were an extra burden to both Kim and Hank Valverde.

Since it was easy to be a bit careless in properly wearing the gear, Top Gordon carried on a methodical and scrutizing jumpmaster check in which he painstakingly inspected each of the Black Eagles — including the higher ranking Major Falconi and Lieutenant Hawkins. This was to minimize the chance of injuries or even death on the drop zone.

Their transport, a huge C-130, appeared in the brightening sky at the same time that both Falconi and Hawkins had completed their inspection by the meticulous Top. Under normal conditions, the aircraft would have arrived the evening before, but the great risk of having it shelled to pieces by Viet Cong mortar squads made it imperative that it spend as little time as possible on Camp Nui Dep's dirt runway.

An Air Force sergeant, shirtless and sweating in the bunker beside the airstrip, directed the big bird in for a faultless landing. Falconi and Hawkins, fully loaded for war, waddled over to the airplane as it wheeled around and had its engines cut by the pilot.

The crew chief opened the door and nodded. "Good morning."

"Howdy," Falconi said looking up. "Is your boss in?"

"I hope the hell he is, sir," the sergeant said, grinning. "He was the one that was supposed to be driving."

A major appeared in the door. "Falconi? Hi there, *paisano*. I'm Carvello. I hope to hell you have a map showing where we're supposed to be going. The missions you guys go on are so damned classified that we don't get any briefing other than being told where to pick you up."

"It's all on a need-to-know basis, and that's further complicated by a time frame. But I have a map for you with the route already plotted for you," Falconi said. He handed over a carefully marked topographical printout. "The drop zone is indicated and they tell me the course is one-three-five, then a turn to oh-twenty-two for the run over the DZ."

Major Carvello took the map and studied it. "Well, you won't be with us long. What's the altitude for your exit?"

"Thirteen thousand over the DZ," Falconi said.

"Right," Carvello answered as he quickly noted the elevation indicated on the map. "I'll pass this info on to my navigator and get the flight lined up. I presume you'll want to tailgate my ship."

"Right," Falconi said. He liked the man's professionalism and obvious experience. He glanced back at his men. Top Gordon was making a check of Blue Richards with only Archie Dobbs left to go. "We'll be ready for station time in five minutes."

Carvello nodded and displayed a snappy salute. "Welcome aboard then, Major."

Chris Hawkins waited as the crew chief dropped the ladder, then quickly ascended it into the aircraft. Falconi, in his usual manner, stood by the door. It had always been the major's custom to be the last aboard, giving each man a wink and a grin as he boarded the aircraft.

Within ten minutes, all thirteen Black Eagles were seated and belted in as the big airplane rolled slowly, then faster and faster, finally picking up the speed necessary to lift itself into the heavy air of Southeast Asia.

Since the flight would be less than forty-five minutes, including the climb to thirteen thousand feet, the pilot cranked open the huge aft cargo doors of the plane. As they opened, a rush of wind and the roar of the engines engulfed the passengers. Falconi's thoughts, as he sat there staring out into the jungle far below, were calm and collected. He had a job to do; the fact that he had to hurl himself out of this aircraft into empty sky in order to commute to it caused him no special excitement. He was as calm as any suburbanite white-collar worker taking the six-fifteen local into the big city to put in his eight hours of paperwork toil.

Falconi's thoughts were interrupted by the crew chief. A silent signal from the Air Force NCO told him that the time was near. The major stood up and motioned to his men to follow as he walked to the edge of the aircraft's open ass-end. There would be no need for formal jump commands in this exit. When the green jump light lit, he would lead his detachment as a compact group out into space for a sixty-second drop through lonely emptiness. They would spread out to put safe distances between themselves during the drop to the earth below. But they had the extra requirement of sticking close enough together to be tactically effective upon landing.

The red light on the bulkhead suddenly glowed and the guys instinctively shuffled forward. Archie Dobbs, situated in the rear of the crowd, had to stand on his tiptoes to see the colored bulb dimly showing in the semidarkness of the fuselage's interior.

Then the green one blinked on.

Archie, who had missed it, was a couple of steps behind his pals as they rushed through the opening and into the clear sky. He literally ran out the door, barely noting the sudden loss of noise of the engines. He was in a clumsy position and caught an upside-down glimpse of the airplane seeming to streak away from him. Archie finally turned himself around and assumed a frog position. He caught sight of the other Black Eagles below him.

Archie's pride was stung.

As the detachment scout, he was always first, even to the point of being ahead of Major Falconi. He'd be doubly-diddly-goddamned if those bastards were going to beat him to the ground. He went head-down into a delta position, with his legs slightly spread and his arms back along his sides. Archie grinned to himself as he went from a fifty-meter-a-second dive to over eighty. He slashed down to the level of the others, then passed them.

The altimeter needle on his reverse spun rapidly as he sped groundward. Then, at fifteen hundred feet, he pulled the ripcord.

He barely slowed down, only seesawing back and forth a bit.

A frantic glance at his parachute showed that the opening sleeve had hung up, holding the canopy closed. This was the dreaded "streamer" so feared by jumpers. He clawed at the reserve ripcord and felt the nylon rush past his feet. At the same time he noted he was at tree-top level.

Then everything—wind, falling, senses, sight, smell—it all suddenly ceased.


The radio operator stretched his small frame within the confines of his net-covered hammock and yawned.

The jungle's awakening animals chattered and called to each other at this beginning of the new day. The man, an ARVN corporal, slipped on his boots and stepped out onto the spongy ground. If his family had been wealthy he could have avoided army service altogether, but his luck was not that good. He had, however, been quite a good student. As a youth he garnered several minor scholastic awards. This proved helpful after he was drafted, and had gotten him a choice assignment to radio operator-technician after basic training. Once again his quick mind served him as he earned an early promotion as a noncommissioned officer after graduation from communications school.

This posting, however, at a lonely jungle site to man a relay station with two other commo men was not the choicest. Their job was to stay tuned to their heavy AN/PRC-47 radio and relay weaker signals from troops operating out in the field back to Camp Nui Dep and even farther if necessary.

They all resented the cruddy assignment and finally agreed between themselves to ignore their radio at night. Instead of sitting up in the dark in miserable wakefulness, they would snooze the nocturnal hours away and get plenty of rest. If some grumpy bastard complained he hadn't been heard, they would simply pretend that his signal had not been picked up.

The soldier glanced at his sleeping companions, deciding not to wake them for a while. He walked over to the tall *doi* tree to check the antenna that was cleverly concealed within its thick bark and strung up into the highest branches overhead. Satisfied it was still intact and not pulled down by some night-prowling monkey or other animal, he walked toward the radio set where it sat protected by a poncho thrown over it.

The soldier looked at his watch to take note of the time, then raised his head in time for the burst of

AK47 fire to blow it apart like a melon ripened too long in the sun.

The other two ARVNs, stupid with sleep, sat up with half-opened eyes. Their ears didn't perceive the thud of the grenade that bounced once on the ground before rolling under their hammocks.

The explosion killed the first outright and wounded the other. He was blown up into the air, his buttocks and the backs of his thighs shredded into hamburger by shrapnel. Shock replaced the previous stupor and he looked straight into the face of the man who now stood over him.

This stranger was not dark, but didn't have Oriental eyes. He seemed European in a strange way, but obviously was not. The soldier winced in pain. "*Curu toi voi*," he pleaded.

His plea for help was answered with the single round of a Kalashnikov assault rifle that blew away his lower jaw. The ARVN rolled over on his back. He felt no pain, but could not comprehend anything either. He simply waited to see what would happen next.

It was another shot in the head — and this one put out the light of life for good.

Maj. Omar Ahmar looked down on the kid he'd just blown away, then slowly shouldered his weapon. He turned back to his men, who had now filtered into the open space of the crude communications center. "*Ajal* — hurry! The radio will be most useful."

The Algerian soldiers quickly cut two long poles from the surrounding vegetation and fixed up a large hammock using the two ponchos that had covered the AN/PRC-47. Then they clumsily gathered up the commo gear, including several of the ten-pound batteries, and threw them onto the crude conveyance.

Ahmar gestured toward the jungle. "*Ruh* — move out!" He watched his eager men disappear back into

85

the vegetation, then looked around once more at the three dead ARVN. The Algerian major was pleased. Their mission for that morning had been quickly accomplished. Higher headquarters would praise them for this important work of destroying the relay station.

It was the same one, well known to Communist intelligence, that was necessary for Major Falconi and his gangsters to use in order to communicate with their home base for aid and support.

Now those running dogs were cut off and isolated, completely at the mercy of Ahmar and his men.


Archie Dobbs could see nothing but a dull, red film in front of his eyes. He tried to speak and sit up, but his nerves were incapable of sending or receiving signals between themselves and the muscles necessary for movement.

Finally, his vision cleared a bit and he perceived a roundish shape in front of his eyes. The red atmosphere slowly faded into normal colors. Things were blurred, but after a while they swam into focus and he recognized the serious expression of Malpractice McCorckel.

"Archie?"

"Huh?"

"How do you feel?"

"Huh?"

"Look. Can you see my fingers in front of your face?" Malpractice asked.

Archie could now plainly see the two fingers, but he couldn't talk. "Huh?"

"How many fingers are there?"

"Huh?"

Malpractice swore under his breath. "Fucking dickhead." Then he tried again. "How many fingers am I holding up, Archie?"

"Huh — uh, eh, two — two — two."

"Alright already!" Malpractice said. "Enough."

Archie felt his friend's fingers probing his neck and around his shoulders. "Queer fucking medic." He grinned and stirred.

"Don't move yet!" Malpractice exclaimed.

"Screw you." Archie struggled up. The pain hit him like giant pincers had gripped his sides. He yelled, but that only increased the hurt.

Then the red film over everything returned.

The last thing he heard was Malpractice's voice that sounded far off. It said, "Damn, sir. Archie's really fucked up."

# Chapter 8

The North Vietnamese army was one that literally looked like hell. It could best be described as drab and ragged with bright little spots of red here and there. The building that housed that army's intelligence bureau mirrored that image perfectly. It was a down-at-the-heels former French government office building of three floors. Neglected, with paint peeling off both the outside and inside, it had a couple of red signs with gold letters on the front that identified it as *Cong-Vu* — Civil Service. Although colorful, this advertisement was an incomplete statement. Too many uniformed men went in and came out, and too many others entered the dreary structure — and disappeared.

The general populace was not really fooled.

Among the men quartered there was a major named Truong Van. For several years he had been assigned to aid a Russian KGB man named Lt. Col. Gregori Krashchenko who had been posted to Hanoi on a very special assignment. Their single, all-encompassing job had been to bring about the destruction of the Black Eagles and the capture of the detachment leader Maj. Robert Falconi.

It was well known to the Communists that Falconi's mother, Miriam Ananova Silberman, had been born in Russia. The fact that she was Jewish and had fled the

Soviet Union to escape persecution was of no consequence. Under the laws of the Workers and Peasants Paradise, not only was she still a citizen of Russia, but so was her son Robert Mikhailovich. That meant that if he were captured, he could be tried as a traitor and executed under the provisions of the Soviet legal system.

Naturally, such an event would be made into a big propaganda show in which Falconi would confess to every war crime in the book including the killing of Cock Robin by wrapping primer cord around his little, feathered neck.

Krashchenko, the Russian, was a most unusual person in Communist society. He was not only alive and kicking, but was not inhabiting a Siberian prison camp despite the fact that he'd fucked up bad — so bad, in fact, he had spent a brief period of time as a prisoner in the south, captured, no less, by the very man he'd been tasked with destroying, U.S. Army Maj. Robert Falconi. After a brief time in an ARVN prison, which included long sessions of "debriefing," Krashchenko had been exchanged for several important prisoners held in the north.

Krashchenko's return to the Commie fold hadn't been something he'd really looked forward to. He figured the best that would happen to him would be a thorough debriefing, then a short walk to the nearest wall to act as a living target for one of the local firing squads.

But his boss, Vladimir Kuznetz, the ranking KGB man in Southeast Asia, recognized that Krashchenko would now really be a highly motivated individual when it came to bringing Maj. Robert Falconi to Soviet justice. Not only would such a deed be rewarded, but it would keep him from being executed. Therefore, Kuznetz had returned Krashchenko to duty and urged him to press ahead to a successful conclusion of his mission.

Krashchenko, relieved and fearful, returned to his task with a vengeance.

This KGB lieutenant colonel had been originally chosen to accomplish the defeat and capture of Falconi because of his previous background. His first years of service to Mother Russia had been filled with glory, promotions, medals and great promise. He'd begun his military career in the Russian army after volunteering to serve in the elite units of the *parachutno-decantye* — the paratroops.

His boyhood was marked by excellent scholastic achievements in school. He carried his natural desire to please his superiors over into the army. As a junior lieutenant, Krashchenko's energetic bootlicking and toadyism quickly caught the attention of his regimental commissar. These special officers were like chaplains in other armies, except they spread the gospel of communism while working hard to bring more sheep into the Red fold.

What pleased this political officer so much was that Krashchenko did more than display a great amount of attentiveness in the classes extolling the virtues of communism and socialism; he went a dozen or so steps further and wrote several treatises expounding the philosophies the commissar preached to the men.

This resulted in favorable reports sent forward praising the eager shavetail's qualities of loyalty to the party. Eventually it was recommended that he be transferred from the role of line officer to the political branch of the Soviet army.

Krashchenko put the icing on the cake himself when he turned in a fellow officer who had been making unpatriotic remarks regarding the institutions of communism and the Soviet government in general. Under normal circumstances, this action would have cinched the political officer's job, but Krashchenko was able to receive even a better advancement — and for a very good reason.

The man he turned in was his own cousin, the son of Krashchenko's favorite aunt.

This brought him to the attention of the KGB, and their probing investigation convinced this Committee of State Security that Lt. Gregori Krashchenko was their kind of guy. In a political system that could not survive or function without brigades of snitching finks and backstabbers, the lieutenant was a godsend to those in authority — even if they were atheists.

The KGB academy proved another feather in his bonnet. He graduated with honors and was rewarded with an exciting assignment of counterinsurgency in the Ukraine. The local peasants, never too fond of their Russian masters, were fighting back in a manner that showed all evidence of soon getting completely out of hand. Krashchenko went after them and proved his deadly efficiency by bringing a detachment of East German police to massacre the Ukranians. Since this was also considered on-the-job training for the Kraut Reds, it proved the fledgling KGB operative's efficiency without a doubt.

Krashchenko's career continued to soar as he turned his attention to other hard cases, and he pursued them straight into the hell of the Soviet concentration camp system without regard for their innocence or guilt.

Finally he received an assignment that was considered a plum. The North Vietnamese had sent disturbing reports to their Russian big brothers about a special detachment of raiders led by an American officer. This enigmatic group had been doing some real damage and immediate help was requested to handle them.

Krashchenko, now a lieutenant colonel, was sent to Hanoi where he teamed up with Maj. Truong Van of the North Vietnamese army G2. This major, an order-of-battle expert, was among the first to properly identify the raiders, so he was assigned to Krashchenko as an assistant and interpreter.

Within six months, utilizing a North Vietnamese agent named Xong and his Saigon organization, they had managed to blackmail a South Vietnamese colonel named Ngai Quang into ferreting out information on this detachment of the Americans' Special Operations Group. Thus, within a very short time, Krashchenko knew all about Major Falconi and his Black Eagles.

When a deep background check on the American officer revealed his curious status with the Soviet government, all stops were pulled to grab him.

But, alas for poor Kraschenko, from that point on, all his plans, aims and operations had gone completely, wholly and undeniably to hell. Not only did his efforts not produce the desired results, they caused the destruction of a North Vietnamese infantry battalion, the end of a planned nuclear reactor in Laos, the loss of an elite detachment of East German police—not to mention the capture of their leader, the obliteration of Xong's intelligence net in Saigon and a complete disruption of operations along the Ho Chi Minh Trail.

Maj. Truong Van, his North Vietnamese aide, had turned quite nasty toward him by then. He had once been respectful and polite to the Soviet officer. But with this mountain of failures, the North Vietnamese officer sneered openly at the Russian, insulting him and even laughing at his efforts.

Truong's attitude sure as hell hadn't changed much since Krashchenko's exchange for other prisoners, but the strange determination in the Russian's demeanor caused him to pause and reflect about any more insults. He finally decided to display a proper, but distant, respectfulness.

Now these two strode down a dingy, long hall on the North Vietnamese Intelligence Headquarters' third floor. After reaching a door, Krashchenko rapped on it and stepped into a spacious, sparsely furnished conference room. Truong followed.

There were four men waiting for them there: Gen. Vladimir Kuznetz, the senior KGB man in the area; Col. Henryk Blinoski of Polish army intelligence; Col. Gyorgy Szako of the Hungarian State Police; and Col. Ngyun Lim, a commissar in the North Vietnamese army. These four comprised a powerful organization initially known as the International Southeast Asian Liberation Committee. But later considerations brought about the shorter name of International Liberation Committee. This was not done for efficiency. Instead, in the event of success, the committee's activities could be directed to other parts of the world other than Southeast Asia — such as the Middle East, Latin America or Africa.

The committee became known by an even shorter appellation. Using the Russian language as initials for their name, they were listed in official Red intelligence agencies by the acronym MOK.

The quartet that directed MOK was seated behind a long, wooden table that faced the door. Two chairs were sitting in front of them. Krashchenko and Truong each took one after rendering snappy salutes.

Kuznetz smoked an evil-smelling Russian cigarette. "Your note said that you had a progress report for us, Comrade Krashchenko."

Krashchenko nodded. *"Da, Tovarisch General.* The Black Eagles are in the operational area now. Observers reported that they parachuted in earlier today."

"Well done!" exclaimed the Hungarian.

General Kuznetz almost sneered. "The only way to infiltrate the territory in question was by parachute. And they were but four acceptable drop zones available there. Keeping surveillance teams on each was no special accomplishment." He looked back at Krashchenko. "I presume there has been no contact with them."

"Not yet, Comrade General. But the radio relay station has been eliminated," Krashchenko reported nervously. The fact that his ass was on the line loomed very large in the back of his mind. "For all intents and purposes, the Black Eagles are isolated and cut off."

The Polish officer clapped his hands. "Surely that is an accomplishment!"

The general shrugged. "We have known of that radio for the previous six months. It could have been eliminated at any time we wished."

The North Vietnamese officer behind the table did not let the Russians' sour disposition spoil his own. "I wish to point out, comrades, that the leader of the Algerian group is a man that I personally chose from the prison population of POWs shortly before the great victory at Dien Bien Phu."

Kuznetz relented a bit. "You are indeed to be congratulated, comrade. Major Ahmar and his men will undoubtedly score an impressive coup in this operation."

"And our struggling comrades in the Viet Cong and North Vietnamese army shall soon have Hungarians and Poles fighting alongside them," Colonel Szako said.

"But first we must get Falconi," Kuznetz reminded him.

"The sooner the better!" exclaimed Blinoski.

Truong, who had sat silently beside his boss Krashchenko, finally spoke. "Allow me to enter a word or two of counsel here. There is no rush to accomplish this task. Hurrying has been the cause of our past failures. We Vietnamese Communists have learned that patient, successful plodding will eventually earn us the world."

"Indeed!" Col. Ngyun Lim agreed.

"You are right, of course," Kuznetz said. "The antiwar demonstrations in the United States have given us the time we need. The American politicians are hesitant about fully committing their country's resources to this struggle. Each day of halfheartedness on their part buys us at least a week more of precious time to fight in our own style."

"It is still imperative that the people's struggle in Southeast Asia becomes an international effort," Szako the Hungarian insisted.

"All of that depends on Ahmar and his Algerian comrades," Kuznetz reminded him. "At any rate, any plan of ours will stand a better chance when Falconi and his gangsters have been removed from the scene."

Col. Ngyun Lim nodded his understanding. "In all my radio transmissions to the Algerians, I emphasize that Falconi must be taken alive."

"Exactly!" Kuznetz exclaimed. He pointed a pudgy finger at the North Vietnamese officer. "The chance to put him on trial in Moscow as both a traitor and a war criminal will be the Communist nations' second greatest propaganda coup of the century. It will rank right after the liberation of Nazi death camps."

"Indeed!" Hgyun agreed.

Kuznetz looked at Krashchenko. "We will expect daily reports from you, comrade."

"Of course, Comrade General."

"And results," the general added ominously. "Excellent results!"

*"Da, Tovarisch General!"*

"You are dismissed."

95

Krashchenko and Truong sprang to their feet and saluted. After executing sharp about-face movements they literally paraded out of the room. The duo didn't relax until they were halfway down the hall.

Truong lit a cigarette as they walked back to their own office. He exhaled a cloud of smoke and asked a pointed question. "Are you optimistic, Comrade Krashchenko?"

"In a special case like this? Of course!" Krashchenko replied with feeling.

"Special?" Truong queried. "It has always been unique and special."

"Not like now," Krashchenko reminded him as he fished out his own pack of cigarettes. "It's either Falconi or me."

Truong smiled. "Quite an incentive, eh, comrade?"

"There is a saying in Russian," Krashchenko said, striking a match. "The hungriest hawk dives the fastest and steepest."

Truong slowed down and watched the KGB man stride rapidly away from him. "Man's greatest instinct is that of survival," he said to himself. "And that could give the Russian sonofabitch that extra drive he needs to finally destroy Robert Falconi."

He took another drag from his cigarette, then hurried after his Soviet companion.

# Chapter 9

Chief Brewster wiped at the sweat that seeped from beneath the camouflage band he had wrapped around his head. He put the radio handset to his ear and pressed the transmission button again. "Abner. Abner," he said tersely. "This is Falcon. Over." After a few moments of waiting, he repeated the effort. "Abner. Abner. This is Falcon. Over."

Falconi shook his head. "Let's give it up, Chief. We've been trying to raise that station for two hours."

"Aye, aye, sir," the Navy chief petty officer answered. "You don't suppose there's been some fuck-up in getting the word down to us, do you? Like that relay radio ain't out here at all. Hell, maybe it never was."

"I know it's in operation, or at least it was a short time ago," Falconi said. "I was in Riley's commo shack a couple of times when they sent messages in from patrols that were out prowling the hinterlands." He looked skyward through the canopy of trees overhead. "It could be that the atmospheric conditions are just right to put any kind of commo completely out of whack right now."

The chief nodded. "That might be it. Even sunspots can affect transmissions if their activity is just right for it." He looked skyward and shrugged. "I doubt it though. There's probably a big screw-up somewheres by the powers that be." Then he slowly shook his head in disgust. "Most likely, though, the lazy ARVN bastards manning the set are fucking off."

"Yeah," Falconi agreed. He turned and glanced down the column formed by the detachment. They were on a narrow trail, but had stepped off it into the jungle during the halt. The major nudged Calvin Culpepper who squatted down just behind him. "Pass the word for Malpractice to come up."

Calvin looked back and whispered back to Kim. The message was relayed from man to man until it reached the medic. Malpractice left his place and walked silently up to his commanding officer. "Yeah, Skipper?"

"How's Archie?"

"We gotta get him medevaced, sir," Malpractice said.

"How important is time?" Falconi asked.

"The sooner, the better," Malpractice said. "If he ain't outta here and under a doctor's care within another twelve hours, he'll croak."

"Jesus!" Falconi said with concern. "It's a miracle the feisty sonofabitch wasn't killed."

"Anybody else who'd taken a thirteen-thousand-foot nosedive would be deader'n a goddamned squashed bug," Malpractice said.

"Any ideas about his exact physical condition?" Falconi asked.

Malpractice sighed. "Hell, I can't tell for sure without X-rays. But it's obvious he's got head and internal injuries. The bleeding from his nose and ears is getting worse. We got to call in a chopper damn quick." He glanced at Chief Brewster. "How's the radio transmitting going?"

The chief shook his head. "Sorry, shipmate."

Malpractice turned his anxious glance back to Falconi. "Archie's gonna die if he ain't taken outta here."

"OK, I understand. Thanks, Malpractice." Falconi watched the medic return to his place in the detachment. "Ray!" he called out to Swift Elk who was located in the opposite direction. The major lit a cigarette and pulled a map from his pocket as he waited for the Sioux Indian to join him and the chief.

Since Archie Dobbs' injury on the parachute jump, Ray Swift Elk had taken over the scouting chores of the detachment. And there was no doubt he looked the part. Rather than wear the black and green face paint like the others did, Swift Elk had applied his in the pattern of war paint used by his ancestors. It had been something passed down to him from his father, who had learned it from his own father, who in turn had learned it from Swift Elk's great-grandfather. That particular gentleman had actually worn the streaks across his face during battles against the same United States Army in which Ray now served.

"Yeah, Skipper?" Swift Elk's copper-colored skin seemed even darker under the facial coloring he wore.

"We're changing directions," Falconi said. He pointed to a spot on the map. "This is where that radio relay outfit is supposed to be. The only way we'll be able to figure out this situation is to call on those bastards. Figure your azimuth and get us there."

"Yes, sir." Swift Elk sat the map on the ground and put his compass on it, aligning the cross hairs with the grid lines. After a turn to allow for the declination, his quick mind mentally calculated distance and direction. He stood up. "Let's go, sir. We got a four-hour walk ahead of us. Are we gonna raise Nui Dep when we get there?"

"Yeah," Falconi answered. "If it's possible."

He signaled back to his men and they quickly got to their feet. Back in the center of the column, Blue Richards and Hank Valverde lifted the field-expedient litter they had constructed. Archie Dobbs lay on it, slipping in and out of consciousness as he murmured softly to himself. Despite his condition, there was a spark alive within his psyche that kept his subconscious mind informed of the fact that he was in a dangerous area. Any loud noises on his part would not only prove deadly to himself, but to his buddies too.

Malpractice took a couple of seconds for another look at his seriously injured patient. He gently wiped Archie's face. "Hang in there, buddy," he whispered.

The Black Eagles moved out with Malpractice walking beside the litter. The concerned medic kept branches and other vegetation from scraping against Archie.

Blue Richards, on the rear of the litter, glanced over at Malpractice. "Are we gonna medevac ol' Archie?" the Alabaman asked.

"Yeah," Malpractice replied. "Either that or bury him."

The people slowly and fearfully gathered around the village square. They maintained a nervous silence as the men who had been working in the fields were brought in under the armed escorts of the soldiers who had suddenly appeared out of the jungle.

The older inhabitants noted something familiar about these unwanted visitors. During the war between the Viet Minh and the French there had been many races of soldiers in their country who served the Tricolor of France. These included white Europeans, black Senegalese and brown men from North African units who looked exactly like these men.

This caused some confusion. This place, called Tinh-Ly-Nho, was the home of peasants who wanted nothing more out of life than to be left in peace to grow their rice, raise their children and live to a dignified old age before crossing into the Great Void after a quiet death. But the ever-present conflicts between strange ideologies kept bringing belligerent strangers into their midst. These unwelcomed visitors harangued them in efforts to persuade the peasants to take sides in something they cared absolutely nothing about.

The situation had forced the people to play a game of sorts with occupying troops. When the Viet Minh were in their midst, the villagers displayed pictures of Ho Chi Minh and responded enthusiastically to the shrill speeches of political commissars. At times that the Europeans showed up, crucifixes and French flags adorned the walls of each and every hovel. With the creation of South Vietnam, they had acquired the proper flags for that army's appearances as well.

But now no one was certain what to do. These new visitors were like those who came in with the French, but they seemed a bit different.

So the village population wisely put on a totally neutral facade in which no banners, photos of leaders or political slogans were displayed. The village schoolteacher and the children stood together where they had been herded. Some of the children began to cry when they found they would not be allowed to join their parents in the crowd. The young schoolmaster kept his charges as calm as possible with reassuring words and smiles. He even picked up and held a couple of the youngsters in his arms who seemed to have a need for some extra attention.

Maj. Omar Ahmar stood at the well in the center of the square, watching as his men pushed and shoved the villagers into a compact group. He could recall similar incidents during his Indochinese tour of duty in the French army when a few cases of rape always occurred. But these young Algerians had been steeped in the absolute necessity of committing no outrageous crimes against the population—unless a certain group opposed them. Then retaliation and atrocities permitted were unlimited.

Finally satisfied that the entire village population was present, Ahmar stepped forward. He greeted them in French, displaying a wide smile. *"Bonjour, peuple de* Tinh-Ly-Nho."

Although a good percentage of the populace spoke and understood that language, a native interpreter attached to the Algerian company translated the words into Vietnamese.

"My men and I have come a long ways to do our share in liberating you from the Americans and their running dogs in Saigon," Ahmar said. "We are part of a grand scheme to create a worker and peasant paradise under the benevolent guidance of Ho Chi Minh. This struggle is shared by others like ourselves outside of Vietnam. We have asked you, the people of Tinh-Ly-Nho, to join us. Brave young men who wish to fight may go with us to a place where they can join the courageous comrades of the Viet Cong. Others, who stay behind, can help by providing food and shelter to the freedom fighters in this people's war against Western imperialism. You may give us information when American and South Vietnamese soldiers come through the area. Tell us how many there are, what direction they came from, what direction they went when they left you, and other valuable intelligence."

The people, who had been listening to these pleas since 1946, nodded agreeably and smiled as they silently wondered when these particular assholes were going to leave. They didn't care what direction, just so the interlopers left!

Ahmar paused. "So. The first thing we want is for all the young men who have the courage to fight for the high ideals of Chairman Ho Chi Minh to step forward and volunteer to serve in the ranks of the brave Viet Cong." He knew there was an undercover VC agent in the village. If necessary the man could identify himself to the Algerians through a password. In the meantime, Ahmar had orders to get soldiers for the Red revolution.

Not one of the people moved. A sense of foreboding settled over the crowd as Ahmar paced back and forth a few times.

"Come now! Don't be bashful. Your family and friends will honor you. Step forward to serve your people."

The crowd stood motionless.

Ahmar's face twitched with anger. "There is undoubtedly someone who has influenced you into a very bad attitude. That situation must be corrected immediately." He gestured at his senior sergeant. *"Jibli kawam fakih!"*

Orders were shouted, and two soldiers rushed to the startled schoolteacher, forcing him to set down the children he was holding. The Algerians dragged him across the square, throwing him down at Ahmar's feet. The major glared at the young man. "What have you been telling these people?"

The teacher attempted to stand up, but the sergeant grabbed him roughly and shoved him down. So he knelt there, looking up at the major. "I only teach the children."

"What do you teach them, schoolmaster?" Ahmar asked. "Do you teach them the glorious teachings of Ho and Mao?"

"I do not speak of the outside world here," the young man said. "These are a simple people who have no interest in political ideology. I only teach their children to read, write and cipher simple sums."

"You are modest, schoolmaster," Ahmar said with a vicious grin. Although he knew for sure that the teacher was innocent of taking anybody's side, he continued on with the object lesson he wanted to instill on the population. "I think you are a big factor in the philosophy and attitude of the Tinh-Ly-Nho villagers. Unfortunately, you are a tool of the imperialists."

"I beg your pardon, *monsieur*, I am only a country schoolteacher."

"We must use you for a positive example," Ahmar said. He pulled out his pistol.

The schoolteacher let his head droop. He knew the situation was hopeless. All his youthful ambitions and high ideals of helping the peasants had come down to this.

Ahmar's Tokarev pistol barked, the 7.62 slug shattering the young man's skull. The victim fell backwards into an undignified heap with his legs under him. He twitched twice, then was still. Ahmar looked from the body to his men. "Now get some volunteers for the Viet Cong. *Kawam!*"

The Algerians pushed their way into the crowd, grabbing young men and hauling them bodily to the front where the corpse of the gentle teacher lay in the hot tropical sun.


Ray Swift Elk stopped and motioned back to Falconi. The major signaled a halt to the column. This allowed the scout to move forward for a recon of the area. The Sioux dropped to all fours and inched forward through the brush without making a sound.

He had spotted the cleared area where the radio relay station was located. Fearing a trap—or even an unintentional shot sent his way by some nervous ARVN soldier—Swift Elk decided that a full investigation was warranted.

He reached the edge of the tree line and peered around the clearing. All was silent except the loud buzzing of insects. Swift Elk knew that sound well. Corpses untended in the hot weather tended to rot quickly and attract huge, obscene blowflies that flew around the dead. The loathsome creatures even landed at times to enter the noses, ears and mouths of cadavers. Swift Elk caught sight of a cloud of the flying bugs at one spot, and another large bunch a few meters away. Carefully, painstakingly, he pulled back into the jungle and began a slow, deliberate circuit of the radio station.

Forty-five minutes later he was back at the starting point. He stood up and motioned to Falconi who, with the rest of the detachment, had been patiently waiting farther back in the dense jungle. "It's clear, Skipper."

The Black Eagles moved in and found the three dead radio operators. There was no time for ceremony. After removing dog tags from the putrid cadavers, the blackened and bloated dead men were given a hasty burial. At the same time a search was mounted for their radio.

Bill Taylor, the Aussie, reported back in. "Sorry, sir. Can't find a bloody blower anywhere about."

Falconi glanced over at the litter where Archie lay. His frustration was expressed with an expletive spoken in a hoarse whisper. "Shit!"

Chief Brewster didn't give up altogether. "Skipper, I helped train radio operators at the ARVN commo classes. One of the biggest problems we had was teaching 'em how to repair busted transmitters."

"Yeah?" Falconi asked.

"Right. It was damned near impossible," the chief said.

"What are you driving at?"

"Well, Skipper," the chief said. "Since the fuckers couldn't fix any that was on the fritz, we always had 'em tote extry ones out when they was in isolated relay stations like this one."

Falconi brightened. "You think there might be one cached around here?"

"I'd bet my favorite tattoo, sir," the chief answered. "And it should be twenty paces dead south of the antenna. That was the rules so's anybody else that came along could find 'em."

"Go for it," Falconi said desperately.

The chief hunted down the tree that held the main antenna. Once he found it, he began taking tiny steps to the rear. "They got little feet," he said as he paced off the distance. When he reached a point he stopped and pulled his entrenching tool from his belt. A few chops at the ground brought the results he wanted. "Here we go, boys!"

Calvin Culpepper and Blue Richards joined him. The trio dug down three feet before they reached a large package wrapped and taped in a heavy plastic covering. Five minutes later, the AN/PRC-47 radio was unwrapped and ready.

Falconi nervously smoked while the chief set up the transmitter. In the meantime, Ray Swift Elk had pulled a map reconnaissance and picked out a good LZ to bring in a chopper.

Finally, Chief Brewster spoke into the microphone. "Slick. Slick. This is Falcon. Over." He waited a couple of beats. "Slick. Slick. This is Falcon. Over." A moment or two passed, then he grinned. "Sir, I've raised Nui Dep."

Falconi smiled in happy relief, dropping the map at his feet. "Call in a medevac at that LZ, Chief."

"Aye, aye, sir!"

The major hurried over to the litter. Malpractice

106

looked up at him. "What's going down, sir?"

"We're calling in a Medevac now," Falconi said. "Good news, right?"

Malpractice didn't show much enthusiasm. "Tell 'em to hurry, for the love of God!"

# Chapter 10

Ray Swift Elk, operating on the point of the column, was forced to move slow through the clinging jungle. But it was more than the thick vegetation that slowed his progress.

The Black Eagles were doubly burdened. Four men at a time were forced to bear extra weight during the three-hour trek from the former radio relay station to the landing zone that Swift Elk had picked out for Archie Dobbs' medical evacuation. All took turns, including Maj. Robert Falconi and Lt. Chris Hawkins, in the carrying of the injured detachment scout and the hundred pounds of extra commo gear and batteries that made up the recovered AN/PRC-47 radio.

This would have been difficult under even normal conditions. But in the environment of the Cambodian jungle — the steamy, energy-sapping heat and the grasping, resisting wall of the brush that blocked every step of the way — the task drained the energy of even those superbly conditioned men. That included Kim, who hid every discomfort behind the inscrutable Oriental mask of his face while he stumbled and perspired bucketfuls of salty sweat.

Half the ordeal ended when Swift Elk called a halt. He walked down the panting, gasping men to the point where Falconi and Chief Brewster were situated. The

Sioux squatted down, whispering as they all did when in enemy territory. "Skipper, I figger we're about fifteen minutes from the LZ."

"Right," Falconi said. He nudged the Seal commo man. "Do your stuff, Chief."

"Aye, aye, sir."

Bill Taylor and Calvin Culpepper had been lugging the radio just behind him. Taylor slipped out of the CY-3700/PRC-47 radio packing case he'd been carrying strapped to his front while Calvin freed himself from the haversack of batteries that he'd attached and balanced on top his rucksack.

Chief Brewster quickly set up the radio while Blue Richards shimmied up a nearby tree with the wire antenna. Once it was in place, the Alabama farm boy lowered himself back to the ground.

The chief hit the transmit button. "Slick. Slick. This is Falcon. Over. Slick . . ."

"Slick. This is Falcon. Over. Slick. Slick. This is Falcon. Over."

The North Vietnamese radio operator turned up the volume on the speaker of the powerful East German FK-1000 radio. "They are broadcasting again, Comrade Colonel," he announced.

Maj. Truong Van quickly translated the statement for the benefit of KGB Lt. Col. Gregori Krashchenko. They both instinctively leaned toward the large array of communications equipment as they heard the voice of Black Eagles' transmission for the second time that day.

"Slick. Slick. This is Falcon. Over."

Truong was confused. "That is another powerful transmission. I thought the Algerian comrades had destroyed the equipment at the radio relay site."

Krashchenko smiled. "No doubt they did. Perhaps I

should explain something to you. As in KGB operating procedures, the capitalists provide an extra set of communications gear to be hidden near stations in remote areas." He sneered openly at his NVA counterpart. "Native operators cannot always master the technical skills necessary to repair complicated communication devices. Falconi and his gangsters have recovered the extra radio." He stopped talking and referred to the American 1:150,000 scale map spread out on the table beside the radio. He laid his finger on the spot where the radio relay station was marked. "They are not far from here. If they wish to have their injured man evacuated as they stated in the first transmission, they have to be near one of these cleared areas."

Truong studied the map. "Yes. They look like excellent landing zones for a helicopter."

Krashchenko started to speak, but more radio traffic interrupted him.

"Falcon. Falcon. This is Slick. Over."

"Slick. This is Falcon. We are one-five minutes from medevac site. We have the grid coordinates. Are you ready? Over."

"Roger," came the affirmative reply. "But advise you to broadcast in the latest code by CW. Over."

"This is Falcon. Bring in medevac on Lima Zulu on Over."

"Roger, Falcon. Go ahead. Over."

Krashchenko grinned in anticipation as he fastened his eyes onto the map like a cobra going after prey. He pulled a note pad and pencil from his shirt pocket.

"This is Falcon. Bring in Medevac on Lima Zulu on grid coordinates one-zero-six-two-five-one-three-one-one-two. Over."

Krashchenko quickly wrote down the numbers.

"Falcon. This is Slick. Medevac chopper to go in on

110

one-zero-six-two-five-one-three-one-one-two. Over."

"Roger. Over."

"Wilco. Out."

Krashchenko's joy turned to determination. He grabbed the Vietnamese radio operator and spoke rapidly in French. "Contact the Algerians." He shoved his scribbled numbers at the man. "Tell them the Black Eagles will be at this location within a quarter of an hour. They must move fast!"

*"Mais oui, Camarade Colonel!"* The man switched the frequency and began the procedure to contact Maj. Omar Ahmar's radio.


Chief Brewster broke down the AN/PRC-47 in a much shorter time than it took to set it up. Blue Richards again went up the tree. This time he came down with the antenna wire in time for the Navy commo man to roll it up and stow it.

At the same time Calvin Culpepper and Bill Taylor's entrenching tools bit into the soft, pungent earth while Chris Hawkins and Chun Kim wrapped the radio set in the heavy plastic wrapping recovered from the original cache. Within moments the equipment was in the freshly dug hole and covered up.

Ray Swift Elk pulled out his machete and expertly slashed out a pattern in the bark of the closest tree. "That won't be particularly noticeable to strangers," he announced, "but it'll damned well let us know that radio set is here."

"Good idea," Falconi said. He walked back into the jungle where Archie lay on his litter. Malpractice McCorckel wiped at the sweat that threatened to seep into Archie's closed eyes. The medic glanced up at his commanding officer. "How's it look, sir?"

"We'll have Archie heading back to civilization in

fifteen or twenty minutes," Falconi said. He glanced at Hank Valverde and Jake Bernstein who had been carrying the litter. "I'll get you guys spelled now."

Jake flexed his biceps in an exaggerated pose. "I'm fine, sir. Just like pumping iron."

Valverde, his Latin pride not letting him admit fatigue, shrugged. "Hell, sir. Wait'll I'm tired."

Falconi admired his men's attitude, but he had to be pragmatic. "We may have to run, and I want fresh bodies toting our boy there. Calvin and Bill Taylor will relieve you."

Top Gordon took a final drag off the cigarette he'd been enjoying. "Are we ready to go?"

"Just as soon as the new litter bearers get back here," Falconi said, heading back to the front of the detachment.

"OK, guys," Top said. "On your feet."


The young lieutenant was so anxious that he manned his radio himself while the regular R/T operator sat nearby, staring off into space with nothing to do. The officer, who commanded the Algerian platoon situated closely around him, licked the sweat off his lip and grimaced in anticipation as the dead air in the receiver hissed in his ear.

Then he perked up.

*"Lion. Lion. C'est Tigre. A vous."*

The Vietnamese-accented French was clearly understandable to the North African subaltern who had spent his student days in Paris as a leftist activist. He quickly answered. *"Tigre. C'est Lion. À vous."*

The message, with the grid coordinates of the scheduled medical evacuation repeated clearly no less than three times, was loud and clear.

The lieutenant repeated the numbers, then ended

the transmission with an impatient, *"C'est Lion. Fin."* He stood up and barked orders at the startled radio operator as he tossed the gear back to him. The four sergeants who commanded the platoon's squads were close enough to hear what was going on. They needed no urging to get their men assembled.

The lieutenant was so happy he could scarcely contain his joy and act like a dignified officer. He pointed to the open area just beyond the tree line a few short yards from their location.

"That field is where the Black Eagles hope to land a helicopter to pick up their injured man! We will prepare a proper reception for the imperialist gangsters!"

The sergeant in charge of the machine guns stepped forward. A veteran who had learned the trade the hard way while determined French airborne forces kept him under constant pressure, he knew that his men and their weapons would be the most important in the ambush.

The response from Nui Dep was quicker than anticipated. The Black Eagles were still closing in on the chosen LZ when the aircraft's rotors could be discerned in the distance. Falconi grabbed the radio handset that Chief Brewer carried. "Chopper. This is Falconi. Over."

The pilot's voice sounded loud and clear as the major pressed the instrument to his ear. "This is the chopper. You guys ready for me to come on in? Over."

"The LZ isn't secured yet," Falconi cautioned him. "We'll need a few minutes. Over."

The pilot wasn't worried. "I hear the patient is in bad shape. I'll come in anyway. Over."

Falconi felt admiration and gratitude toward the brave pilot. "Roger, chopper. We'll be in the open

113

within five minutes. Out." He handed the handset back to the chief and turned toward the Alpha Fire Team. "Chris!" he called out. "Get your boys to cover the south side of the field. Take Ray with you."

Chris Hawkins wasted no time in rushing to the job with Swift Elk and Kim. The other two members of his team, Calvin and the Aussie, Bill Taylor, were acting as litter bearers for Archie.

Top Gordon quickly came forward with his Bravo Team. Again Falconi wasted no time. "Top, send Blue up with the Alphas. Then take the rest of your team and hold the north side of the LZ."

"Yes, sir," Top replied. Blue, hearing what was wanted of him, had already rushed off to join up with Chris' Alphas. Top took the remainder of the Bravos to their security positions.

"Drop your gear, Chief, but hand over the radio," Falconi said. "I'll call in the chopper, then you and I are going with the litter and give 'em some cover."

"Aye, aye, sir!" He shook himself free of his equipment and passed the radio over to Falconi.

Calvin and Bill Taylor, with the litter between them, came up. Calvin was eager as always. "Let's git ol' Archie outta here, Skipper."

"OK! Let's go, guys," Falconi said.

Within only five minutes, a swift-flying Hughes OH-6A streaked in over the tree line, then slowed and swung around. It came to a roaring hover, then slowly eased toward the ground.

Then the far woods exploded with automatic fire. Rounds clipped the grass and a few sparks leaped from the chopper's fuselage. The pilot wasted no time in hauling ass back up into the sky. His voice, surprisingly amused instead of angry, came over the chief's radio. "Falcon, you weren't just whistling Dixie when you said the LZ wasn't secured, were you? Want me to

114

come back down? Over."

"Stay outta the way, chopper," Falconi said. "We've got to find those bad guys or this will be a big waste."

Ray Swift Elk had followed his natural instincts at the first unfriendly burst of fire. He went to the ground, but not before noting the direction the bad guys were shooting from. He put his M16 on full auto and hosed several rounds in that direction.

Chun Kim crawled through the thick grass and joined him. "Where they at, Ray? I don't see them."

Swift Elk pointed. "That way. They seem to be packed together pretty close for some reason. Unload some o' that artillery o' yours at 'em, Kim."

"Damn betcha!"

In the meantime Chris had also joined them and, also on full automatic, added his volume of firepower to Ray's. Kim slipped a forty-millimeter grenade into the M79 and expertly set the sights. "One round on the way!" He pulled the trigger, and the missile arced into the air to fall in the tree line.

The explosion cut the incoming fire, indicating a direct and lucky hit on one of the enemy machine guns.

Chris slapped the Korean marine on the shoulder. "Don't quit while you're ahead. Keep pumping those babies in."

"OK, by God!" Kim yelled. He wasted no time in going to work.

Top Gordon and his men, on the other side of the landing zone, took advantage of the diversion set up by the Alphas to do some fancy firing and maneuvering of their own. Hank Valverde performed the grenadier chores to add to Kim's devastation.

Sweeps of M16 fire raked the positions until the opposition's fusillades slacked off to a few stubborn spasms of bullets.

Falconi figured the time had come. "Chopper. This is Falcon. C'mon in! Over."

"Wilco!"

The helicopter, which had been orbiting the area at a high altitude, dived down and repeated his initial hovering. The pilot could see the litter bearers and two armed escorts moving onto the LZ. He eased toward them, closing in until finally he dropped to his skids.

The litter was shoved inside and Calvin Culpepper followed it. He quickly lashed Archie to the deck with the cargo straps, cinching them up tightly. He looked at the pilot and gave him a cheery thumbs-up signal, then leaped back outside.

The chopper shot upward, clearing the area. As the Black Eagles moved toward the enemy positions, the noise of the aircraft's motor faded to nothingness.

Ray Swift Elk, leading Chris and Kim, had reached a point on the enemy's right flank. Chris talked quickly to Top on the Prick Six. "Those guys are bunched together. They make one hell of a target. Give me a good twenty-second salvo, then lift it. We'll be going in for the kill. Over."

"You got it, Alpha," Top said on his own radio. "Then we'll join you."

The volley of bullets and grenades stormed the enemy at almost the exact instant. Then the firing stopped.

Ray Swift Elk leaped to his feet and charged forward, his M16 still on full automatic. He emptied a fresh magazine with controlled firebursts of five and six rounds as Chris and Kim followed. The three formed a "V" with the Sioux Indian at the point.

Meanwhile, Top and the other Bravos came in from the other side. Between the two Black Eagle fire teams, a deadly crossfire slapped and kicked at the remnants of the Algerian platoon.

By the time Falconi and the chief arrived it was over.

Ray Swift Elk spat. "Bunch o' fucking amateurs," he said, turning over the body. "They musta been scared or something from the way they hung together."

Malpractice McCorckel called from a short distance away. "They look like a bunch o' kids. No experience."

Top lit a stogie. "Well, the sons of bitches ain't gonna get any either."

Falconi knelt down and examined the nearest dead man in the tan uniform. "Well, guys. Looks like we found those Algerians."

"Bloody good!" the Aussie, Bill Taylor, exclaimed. "Just the blokes we was looking for."

Falconi looked at one of the bodies. "From where this guy fell, it looks like he was directing things. He's probably the platoon leader." He pulled a Black Eagle beret shield from his pocket and laid it on a corpse.

Calvin Culpepper shook his head. "That'll piss 'em off enough to really come looking for us, Skipper."

Falconi nodded. "And that, my friend, is the name of this game."

# Chapter 11

Archie had been safely Medevaced thirty-six hours previously. The intrepid scout, barely conscious, was only dimly aware of the exploding turmoil around me. He'd tried to respond to the stimuli of detonating grenades and bursts of small arms fire, but had only managed to roll around on the litter, making it more difficult for Calvin Culpepper and Bill Taylor as they rushed him across the deadly open space to the waiting helicopter.

The Black Eagles, now prowling the jungle, had stayed at the landing zone long enough to give the enemy dead a thorough searching.

They had found nothing.

Ray Swift Elk, as the intelligence sergeant, did the bulk of the unpleasant task as flies and other insects became attracted by the scent of death that built up quickly in the heat. Finally, after going through the pockets of the last corpse, he stood up and looked over at Falconi with a shrug. "These fuckers are sterile, Skipper. Not a shred of ID or nothing. The maps they got are American and the writing on 'em is French." He carefully scrutinized one, then threw it down in angry disappointment. "There's no evidence of organizations, headquarters — nothing."

Falconi nodded. "I didn't expect to find anything,

Ray. The last things the Reds want are for us to be able to make any positive identification on these guys or be able to find out where their base camp might be."

Swift Elk retrieved his M16 that was leaning against a nearby tree. He swung the weapon up on one muscular shoulder. He took another look at the dense formation of corpses. "The dumb bastards sure packed themselves in tight on this end of the landing zone," he remarked with professional criticism. "I reckon the only thing we know for sure is that this ain't all of 'em."

"That just leaves us with one thing to do," Falconi said. "Find the rest."

"Then let's go get 'em, sir," Swift Elk said.

"My thought exactly." Falconi waved over to Chris and Top. "Let's move out."

The Black Eagles, with Swift Elk at the point followed by the Alphas and the Bravos with Falconi and the chief between the two fire teams, set out to complete the task assigned to them:

Find the enemy, close with and destroy them.


Krashchenko cursed under his breath. "*Glupi Arabka*—stupid Arabs!"

Truong, seated by the big East German radio set, calmly lit a cigarette and glanced over at his Russian colleague. "Perhaps we have no report because of equipment failure in the field."

Krashchenko nervously wiped at the perspiration beading on his forehead. As ever, he was the eternal pessimist. "No! No! They have let a grand opportunity slip past them." He pulled his own cigarettes from his shirt pocket and jammed one in his mouth. He paced back and forth as he touched a match to it. "It is only out of desperation that Mother Russia has linked herself up with them!" he hissed angrily. "All of the dumb bastards together cannot even defeat little Israel!"

Truong poured himself a cup of the tepid tea from the pot that sat between him and the radio operator. "The Algerians won a victory against the French," he countered a bit testily. He hated the Russian's arrogance and superior attitude.

"Bah! If the French nation had put their entire resources into the Algerian war, the place would still be *Algerie Français.*" He turned and sneered at Truong. "The same would have happened here if the government of France had pulled all stops to keep Indochina within their imperialist sphere." He motioned around the room. "This building would still be filled with their chattering bureaucrats."

Truong's eyes clouded over with anger. All the resentment and hatred he'd kept under close wraps boiled up through his Oriental quiescence. "Do not dare to belittle the accomplishments of others while you fail miserably at attaining your own goals, Comrade Lieutenant Colonel Krashchenko! It's only a matter of time before you're under the gunsights of a firing squad!"

Krashchenko spun on his heel and glared at him. He pointed a shaking finger. "Before I go to the wall, you slant-eyed toad, I'll blow your pea-sized brain apart with a bullet from my Tokarev!"

"I thank you for the warning," Truong said. "It only serves to further convince me of your desperation and treachery. I shall always be on guard." He laughed. "Your fate rests on the actions of those—" he paused, then emphasized the words so much that the sarcasm seemed to drip from them—"*glupi Arabka.*"

The Russian took a final drag on his cigarette, then dropped it to the wooden floor where black burn marks from other discarded smokes marred the slats. He pointed to the Vietnamese radio operator. "Tell that idiot to turn up the sound on the speaker."

"Tell him yourself, you Russian racist!" Truong snapped. "He understands French."

The KGB man knew he was beginning to show the strain he was under. This sign of weakness stung his pride. Calming down some, he lit another cigarette and resumed the long period of waiting.


Blue Richards was the best tree-climber in both the Black Eagles and the state of Alabama. He'd developed the skill in his home state while serving as lookout while his grandpappy and pappy worked the family still. Several generations of the Richards family had devoted considerable time to cooking up potent batches of white lightnin' whiskey — guaranteed to both boil your brain and remove paint with equal ease.

Blue now practiced the skill high in the branches of a *soai* tree, his eyes glued to the binoculars as he surveyed the activities of the village which was entirely within his view.

Falconi's map identified the small hamlet as Tinh-Ly-Nho. The intelligence reports that Ray Swift Elk was able to get hold of further described the place as pacified. But both the Sioux and his boss knew that description wasn't carrying any sort of guarantee of veracity. It was just one side's opinion. The Viet Cong might also consider the populace trustworthy. That would mean that the people there, like in many villages, played ball with whomever happened to be present at any particular time.

While Blue continued his tree-top vigil, other members of the detachment had concealed themselves along the three main trails that led from the jungle into Tinh-Ly-Nho. Their mission was not one of ambush, only

121

reconnaissance and observance. There was a good chance, if the intelligence report was correct, that the village could be used as a base camp of sorts. This would be much better than establishing one in the crushing wilderness of the monsoon forest.

Finally, as the sun reddened to begin its rapid descent over the western tree line, Blue slipped his binoculars back into their case and carefully descended his natural perch to the ground far below. He hurried to the quickly established CP to report in to Falconi. He found the fire team leaders, Top Gordon and Chris Hawkins, there too. He nodded to them, then turned his attention to the major.

"I din't see nothin', Skipper," Blue said. "The folks there was just tendin' to their chores."

"Did anyone appear who might be strangers?" Falconi asked.

"No, sir. Ever'body seemed to know ever'body else, and I din't see no weapons either," Blue said. "I kept my eyes out for any fellers that might just be sittin' around like they was VC keepin' a eye on things, but they wasn't nobody like that."

"What about the young guys?" Top asked. "What were they doing?"

"All of 'em went out to them rice paddies on the other side of the village. I could see most o' that area too." Blue pulled a canteen from its carrier and drained what was left in it. "I gotta git some more water. I caught a lotta sun up in them top branches."

Chris Hawkins handed over one of his own full canteens. "Were all those guys working in the paddy, or just standing around like they were on guard?"

"They was workin', Mister Hawkins," Blue said, falling back into Navy vernacular. "Up to they asses in mud."

Falconi took note of the growing darkness. "We'll

122

make contact tomorrow." He pointed to the team leaders. "You guys set up for a quick retreat along the south trail if we need it. I'll go in and talk to the head man with Ray and Chief Brewster."

Top Gordon slowly shook his head. "I don't trust none of the people in this part of the world."

Blue Richards handed Chris back his canteen. He glanced at the master sergeant. "Hell, you cain't blame 'em, Top. Things is tough for 'em."

"That won't make me feel any better if they kill me, or help somebody else perform the honors," Top said dryly.


Archie Dobbs sat up in the bed and looked at the doctor who stood beside it. Archie grinned despite the pain he felt. "I guess you'll be kicking me outta this cushy place pretty damned quick, right?"

The doctor peered at the patient over the medical report he was holding. "Not for a hell of a long time. Your name is Dobbs, huh? Mine is Doctor Davenport." He pulled one of the X-rays and held it up to the light. "Did that damned parachute open at all?"

"Oh, hell, yes!" Archie lied. He laughed and fought the spasms of pain it caused. "I just landed a little hard, that's all."

"According to the report radioed in from the field, you fell thirteen thousand feet," Davenport said. "But I'll be damned if the only physical evidence you have of striking the ground are broken ribs and bruises."

Archie was worried. "Then what's the problem?"

"X-rays don't always give the whole story," the M.D. explained. "Everything from your brain to your intestines got a thorough whacking. We won't know the extent of the damage until you've been through several weeks of tests and observation."

"Bullshit, Doc," Archie said. "Let me outta here."

"You're in pain right now, aren't you?"

Archie shrugged—and it hurt—but he forced a grin. "Not a bit."

Davenport closed the report and rehung it on the end of the bed. He walked around to the side and looked down at Archie. "I'm going to level with you, Dobbs. I don't give a damn about your gung-ho attitude. So don't try to bullshit me into sending you back before you're ready for duty—if you'll ever be. I'm a doctor and a real civilian at heart. My job is to cure you dumb bastards, not rush you back into hell. You have probably hurt yourself to the extent that you're going to have physical problems from it for the rest of your life."

"Yeah, but—"

"Shut up, Dobbs." Davenport called to the nurse who was down at the other end of the ward. "Lieutenant Pembelton!"

"Coming, Doctor," she called back.

When she walked up to the bed, Archie noticed she was a cute little number with red hair and big tits.

Davenport pointed to the patient. "This man must be available for a series of tests starting tomorrow morning."

Archie smirked. "Aw, bullshit! I—"

Davenport's temper snapped. "Listen, buster! You're lying there in that bed in pain. You probably don't know it, but you're also sedated, though you're relatively wide awake. What that adds up to is that you've been injured bad enough to still feel so much discomfort you can't sleep when you should be snoozing like a day-old baby. If I may fall back into your own colloquialisms, Sergeant, you are fucked up—*fucked up!*" He looked back at the nurse. "We've got him on nonconvulsive sedatives. I also want an IV set up for epinephrine solution before he goes into shock, or—" he glared at Archie—"dies of terminal stupidity."

"Yes, Doctor," the cute nurse said. "I'll get one of the ward medics to set up the IV now."

"Hey!" Archie shouted. "You ain't sticking no needles in me. I ain't got the clap!" He started to raise up, but suddenly the world whirled and twisted around him and the red cloud descended over his eyes.

The nurse instinctively reached out a hand and laid it on Archie's brow. "Poor soldier!"

"Are you getting a crush on this guy, Pembelton?" the doctor asked, displaying a wide grin.

Her face reddened. "Of course not, Doctor!"

"I'll tell you one thing about him," Davenport said. "That is a real crazy fucker!"


Torchlight danced over the pile of bodies laid out on the edge of the landing zone. Maj. Omar Ahmar's face was black with rage.

He was as angry with himself as he was with the dead lieutenant who lay at his feet. He knew he should never have separated his command, but it had really been necessary in order to make contact with the capitalist gangsters. The remaining members of the Algerian detachment stood in a semicircle around the dead men, staring in silent dismay at the massacre.

"This is an example of why you must learn to think fast and be adaptable to any situation," Ahmar said. "Most of our training and combat experiences have been ambushes in thick jungle terrain. It is necessary to maintain a close-packed formation in such areas where there is limited visibility."

The men, still numbed by the devastating loss, shifted uncomfortably, but listened intently. Whatever terrible mistake was made here was certainly not going to be repeated as far as they were concerned.

Ahmar pointed to the wide-open landing zone with a sweep of his hand to emphasize its spaciousness. "But out there, the enemy had plenty of room to maneuver. Our dead comrades should have spread out and covered the area with the machine guns situated for good crossfire. Instead, they gathered in tightly and represented a small, compact target in which the imperialists poured a murderous, concentrated fire."

The young Algerians nodded their understanding. Quick glances from the thick copse of trees out to the open area in front of it clearly gave indication that the dead platoon should have been widely dispersed with carefully designated fields of fire to cover the entire LZ.

"But do not worry, comrades," Ahmar continued as he changed his tone to punch some encouragement into his shaken troops. "Our dead will be avenged! Their martydom for socialism shall not go unanswered." He held up a small, shield-shaped insignia: an eagle, grasping a lightning rod in one talon and a sword in the other. "This insulting device was left by the killers on the chest of our dead comrade lieutenant. It is the insignia of the Black Eagles—the worst gangster ever produced by the cancer of imperialist capitalism. With this gesture they have challenged us."

An excited young Algerian waved his AK47 in the air. "We will avenge the blood of our comrades with ten times the amount from the Black Eagles!"

A resounding cheer rose from the assembled companies. Shouts for *intikam*—vegeance—soon evolved into a chant until the entire Algerian detachment clapped their hands and shouted in unison:

"*Katal-Aswad-Isr! Katal-Aswad-Isr!* Kill the Black Eagles! Kill the Black Eagles!"

Ahmar stepped aside and motioned his radio operator to follow him. He would let the sergeants lead the rally that would make his men's thirst for vengeance become nearly insatiable. The major's own duties were more practical. He had to radio through relay to Hanoi for all the guidance and instructions they could give him on closing in with the Black Eagles.

He wasted no time. *"Tigre. Tigre. C'est Leopard. A vous."*

Between them and the Viet Cong intelligence net in the area, there was no fear of failure. Particularly since his command still outnumbered the Black Eagles by twelve to one.

# Chapter 12

The young man stood in front of the hut as his mother poured clear water over his feet to wash away the thick mud picked up during the long day's labor in the rice paddy.

This farmer, named Ngwan, watched the old lady clean him, then lifted his eyes and looked over into the village square. His heart filled with hatred at the sight of the soldiers there.

They had entered Tinh-Ly-Nho early that morning, their American uniforms clearly identifying what side they were on in the war. Their leader, Major Falconi, assured the head man that they would not stay long and would take nothing. The American officer even promised that his men would be well behaved. At least that was true. The only problem was the villagers had to put up with the usual questioning about Viet Cong activity in the area.

This interrogation had been done in a polite and courteous manner, and these soldiers ate their own food and did not steal or loot. They were also respectful toward the women, but Ngwan felt loathing, fear and hatred for them.

When his mother had at last cleaned his feet, the young farmer went inside the hut. His wife sat in one corner humming to herself and thinking whatever thoughts flitted through the foggy blankness of her mind.

Ngwan's wife Kha hadn't always been in that mental condition. At one time she was the prettiest, wittiest and happiest girl in Tinh-Ly-Nho. He'd been extremely proud when his parents had been able to arrange his marriage with her, because most of the young men wanted her and were willing to make a lot of sacrifices in the marriage price to get her. It had ended as a toss-up, so Kha was given the unusual option of choosing between three men as her husband. She'd chosen Ngwan.

Their marriage had been a happy one. But not long after their son was born, their life turned into a hell. A South Vietnamese military police unit arrived at Tinh-Ly-Nho to check the place out for Viet Cong. These men were not regular field soldiers, but a unit of MPs that generally dealt with black marketeers, narcotics dealers and other scum bags on city streets and in back alleyways. They went about their investigation of the village in the same highhanded, ruthless manner they used on criminals in Saigon.

The commanding officer and his first sergeant were the first ones to catch sight of Kha. She was taken to their command post at the jungle's edge for questioning like others had been done. But instead of being released, she'd been held for three days. The ordeal she'd endured had been seventy-two hours of periodic rape by the officer. When his sexual appetite was appeased, he'd turned her over to the first sergeant, who had then passed her on down the line until practically every one of the hundred men in the unit had forced himself on her at least once.

Kha survived. That is, her body survived. The lacerations healed, the bruises faded away and the bites on her neck and breasts finally disappeared. But her mind paid the full price. The experience turned her into a vegetable. She ate and slept, but could do nothing else. Even Ngwan's tender touches would set her off screaming and thrashing as pictures of the countless men looming over her returned.

The next visitors who came to the village were the Viet Cong. They were surprised that this time someone actually stepped forward and volunteered to serve with them against the South. This was the rice farmer Ngwan. When the VC commandant got the full story, he knew he had one hell of a good man for his cause. The man pondered whether to bring Ngwan along and shove an AK47 in his hands, or use him for some subtler but more useful duties. He contacted his next higher-up for advice, and a decision was made that turned the village peasant into an auxiliary.

An auxiliary in guerrilla warfare rarely fights openly with the partisans. He stays in the towns and countryside carrying on his regular life while devoting a great deal of time to the side he serves. He provides intelligence, a safe house, medical aid and other help the fighters need.

It was an open secret when Ngwan began aiding the Communist guerrillas. None of the other villagers dared speak about it among themselves, much less with the South Vietnamese and other units who called on them from time to time. They desired nothing more than to live their own lives and be left in peace. If Ngwan wanted to choose sides, let him. They would only pray that his action would bring no terrible consequences on Tinh-Ly-Nho.

Ngwan took another look at the soldiers, then went inside his hut. His mother gave him a bowl of rice and bits of fish. The young farmer ate his meal, looking over at the vacant face of Kha now and then. Afterward, he went back outside and squatted in the dirt to

130

enjoy his pipe until it became dark. After one more hate-filled glare at the visiting soldiers, he went inside seemingly to retire for the night.

But Ngwan did not sleep. He lay wide awake for several hours. Finally, when the village was wrapped deep in the cloak of the night, Ngwan stood up from his sleeping mat and pushed it aside. He lifted up the trap door in the floor beneath it, sliding into the tunnel entrance below the hut. There was barely a sound as his mother closed the door and slid the mat back over it.

Ngwan rapidly crawled down the tunnel to the end that opened up fifty yards into the jungle. Once outside, he wasted no time in heading for his Viet Cong contact.


Chuck Fagin stepped through the door of the quonset hut and glanced down the row of beds before going to the ward office. He rapped on the partition and looked in. He started to speak, but the sight of the red-haired nurse with large breasts startled him. Fagin cleared his throat. "Hi ya."

The nurse glanced up. She wore a fatigue uniform that bore her insignia and a name tag that identified her as Pembelton. The man in civilian clothes looked out of place. "Yes?"

Fagin produced his ID card. "I'd like to see Staff Sergeant Archie Dobbs. Is it OK?"

"I'll have to clear it with Doctor Davenport first."

Fagin smiled and shoved his CIA credentials closer. 'I really have to speak to him."

Nurse Pembelton was a bit shook up. "Well—yes. I'll go with you to see if he's awake."

"With Archie, it's hard to tell," Fagin said.

Archie Dobbs was indeed alert when they arrived.

He leered at Pembelton, then turned his attention to Fagin. "OK, Chuck. Get my ass outta here, huh?"

"I already tried, Arch," Fagin said. "No deal. You must've really smacked that ground."

The nurse took Archie's pulse, then laid a hand on his forehead. The Black Eagle smiled and looked up into her eyes. "I love you."

Surprisingly, the young woman broke into giggles. "Sometimes you're so cute, I—" She suddenly realized what she was saying. "Your pulse is erratic, but there doesn't seem to be any fever. At least you're not hot enough to take your temperature."

"I'm hot, baby," Archie said. "Hot with desire for you."

Pembelton laughed again, then sobered her expression and spoke to Fagin. "You really shouldn't stay long."

"I'll keep it as short as I can," Fagin promised. He watched the nurse walk away and turned back to Archie. "I think she likes you."

"O'course she does," Archie said. "All the women are wild about me."

"Sure, guy," Fagin said. "I'm supposed to be here to debrief you, but I think I already know more than you."

"Prob'ly," Archie agreed. "All I can tell you is that we jumped outta that airplane. Ever'thing after that is a blank except for jumbled sights and sounds that don' mean much. How are the boys doing?"

Fagin shook his head. "I don't know much. The relay station they were supposed to use is gone, but they've got a radio that can reach Nui Dep. I'm not sure what type it is, but I'm sure they can't lug the damned thing all over the jungle."

"They would cache it for later use then," Archie said impatiently. "Standard procedure. What I'm interested in is being re-inserted into the mission. Can you work

132

that out for me?"

Fagin shrugged. "Sure. I can get you pulled out of here anytime, but I'm not going to do it."

"Why not?"

"For a couple of reasons," Fagin said. "I don't know where Falconi and the boys are, and in your condition you'd be more of a burden than an asset to the detachment. You might even cause somebody to get zapped."

"Bullshit!"

"I'm not going to argue with you," Fagin said. "I have to get through your debriefing session, then back to my office. You'll notice it's night outside."

"Sure, Chuck," Archie said sarcastically. "I hope I ain't keeping you from some social engagement."

Fagin ignored the barb. "OK, guy. Let's get on with this. First question is, what time did you infiltrate the operational area?"

Archie thought a moment. "It was after dawn, and everything was on schedule, so I'd guess we went in about 0500 or 0515."

Fagin grinned. "You were about a minute or so ahead of everybody else to the ground, right?"

Despite his anger and disappointment, Archie smiled back at him. "Yeah I suppose I was."

"OK," Fagin said. "Next question . . ."


Ngwan had to move slowly through the dark jungle. The trail he followed was one he'd gone over many times during daylight hours, and that helped him now since he knew every turn and dip along the way. But the real reason for his ability to move in the complete blackness of the night was his Viet Cong trainers who had made him go that same route while heavily blindfolded. They'd known that most of the time he would need to deliver an important message, it would be during the safer hours of darkness.

Ngwan kept one hand in front of his face to avoid walking into the painfully sharp thorns or branches of the brush. Each step he took was deliberate, as he set his feet gently to the ground to feel for twigs or other debris that might crack or rustle. Only when he was satisfied there would be no noise would the rice farmer allow the full weight of his body to shift to that foot.

It took two hours of this tortuous journey before he reached his destination. A soft-spoken command stopped him. Ngwan wasted no time in giving his code words.

*"Com."*

Ngwan quickly went from that guard to another situated deeper into the interior of the VC camp. Finally he was brought before the awakened commandant. The man didn't even bother to speak even casual salutations. "You have information for us?"

"Yes, comrade. There are twelve enemy soldiers in Tinh-Ly-Nho," Ngwan said.

The commandant shrugged. "They will probably be gone tomorrow some time."

Ngwan shook his head. "I do not think so, comrade. They are on foot and carrying heavy gear. It appears they are participating in an operation or mission of sorts here. They have even asked us about the Africans."

The commandant's eyes widened. He'd been alerted about such a situation. *"Cam on ong*—thank you, comrade. You must return to the village and be there before daylight. We do not want them to know that you have snuck off."

"Yes, comrade," Ngwan said.

"Keep a sharp eye on those gangsters," the commandant ordered. "If they leave, try to follow a bit to see for sure which direction they took. This is very important if we are to intercept them."

"I understand," Ngwan said.

"My men and I will be after the interlopers at the first opportunity," the officer said.

Ngwan stood up and allowed himself to be escorted back to the edge of the camp. Once there, he began the slow journey down the trail back to Tinh-Ly-Nho.


Despite Archie Dobbs' condition, he'd used his natural instincts of direction and orientation to figure the exact layout of the ward. He'd learned the location of his clothes and boots by simply listening to conversations and observing the comings and goings of other patients who had gotten well enough to be granted twelve-hour passes.

Gleaning such information for Archie Dobbs was as natural to him as breathing. The young man was a born tracker and pathfinder.

If he had come into the world a couple of hundred years previously, the intrepid staff sergeant would have been among the first to break across the Appalachian or Allegheny Mountains and move west to explore the dangerous wilderness that spread out from the narrow seaboard of civilization across the unknown sprawl of the American continent. Archie's ancestors, who had arrived in the colonies during the times when such activities were feasible, had been prevented from becoming pioneers due to the circumstances of their arrival.

They had come in chains, released from English prisons as bonded servants—virtual slaves to the people who held the papers on them. Any attempt to leave the supervision and control of their masters was a serious crime. Confused and locked into a cruel system, they had bided their time. When the terms of enslavement ended, they chose to remain within the confines of familiar territory rather than wander off. After a couple of generations, the former bonded servants, through circumstances brought on by the industrial revolution, were caught up in the manufacturing syndrome and life-style of the East Coast.

Thus, the Dobbs—like many other families—donated several generations to the mills and factories of Massachusetts.

Archie's older ancestors in England had been involved in more romantic activities to earn their bread. In fact, it was because of their mode of making a living that they ended up in the English judicial system that eventually sold them into bondage in the colonies.

The Dobbs family were poachers.

No earl, duke, lord of a manor, or even the king of England could keep the persistent Dobbs clan from hunting and fishing their private domains. Generations of following this dangerous trade had developed genes in which the necessary skills of stealth, tracking and directional orientation had evolved to the maximum.

These talents were combined with stubbornness and fearlessness too.

To this day in the English county of Nottinghamshire there is the tale out of the misty past which involves a man named Dobbs who, rather than shrieking in agony while being drawn and quartered, shouted of how he had enjoyed a lord's roasted venison—the very crime for which he was being so painfully executed.

Now the scion of that great line of interloping outdoorsmen—with broken ribs and badly shaken innards—eased himself over the side of the Army hospital bed in the darkness of the ward. A wave of nausea and dizziness swept over him and he gripped the edge of the nightstand to keep from falling. Finally, his head relatively clear, Archie took a few tentative steps toward the center aisle.

Once there he rested again, then began walking toward the end of the ward where the patients' regular uniforms were stored. He was halfway there when he realized he wasn't going to make it. Only blind stubbornness kept him going for another half dozen steps before he pitched forward headfirst to the concrete floor.

Lights came on and the nurse rushed from the ward office. She saw the man in the blue GI pajamas sprawled across the floor. She went to him and knelt down. Once again he was bleeding from his ears and nose.

"Oh, lord!" she exclaimed. "Why are the cutest ones the worst behaved?"

# Chapter 13

Jake Bernstein lay in the shallow fighting hole he'd scraped for himself to use as an impromptu sentry post during the dark hours of the previous night. It was a bit elaborate in that he'd created a small earthen shelf on which he'd placed a fragmentation grenade in case it might be needed.

Ten meters away, similarly situated, Hank Valverde passed his time off guard with intermittent dozing.

Dawn, red and hot, glowed through the trees to the east, casting shadows through the monsoon forest. Several hours previously, the two had thought they sensed someone — or something — moving toward them in the dark. There was no doubt that there had been movement past them. A slight rustling of leaves caught by their alert ears gave away the interloper. But whether it had been a man or animal, neither was sure. Hank gave the alarm to the interior guard team by pressing rapidly several times on the Prick-Six radio's transmit button to break the hiss in the receiver ear port. But there had been no problems in the village, so the insignificant disturbance was passed off as some night-prowling animal looking for prey.

None of the Black Eagles knew it, but the source of this bit of bother had been the peasant Ngwan returning from his sojourn to the VC camp. His presence had not been fully detected since he'd re-entered the tunnel going to his hut and returned through the man-made cave to his crude domicile.

The day glowed brighter now, and Hank came fully

awake. He crawled over and joined Jake at his position. "I guess we sounded a false alarm last night," he whispered. "Makes me feel like a goddamned silly-assed recruit."

Jake nodded his head. "Yeah," he acknowledged under his breath. "But something moved out there. No doubt about that."

"I suppose it was better to alert everyone even—" Hank suddenly shut up.

Jake heard it too. It was the undeniable rustling of vegetation, like a slow-moving water buffalo, easing toward them.

Hank spotted the khaki uniforms first. He brought up the muzzle of his M16 and cut loose. Jake wasted no time in adding his own contribution to the fusillade with several automatic firebursts of a half dozen rounds.

The Algerian advance scouts caught the brunt of the volleys and went down like scythed wheat. Their comrades behind opened up immediately, filling the air with whistling 7.62-millimeter slugs from their Kalashnikovs.

The two Black Eagles ducked as the air zinged with both flying and ricocheting bullets. Jake grabbed his grenade from its little dirt shelf and tugged the pin loose. The spoon popped free and he waited a couple of beats before heaving it toward the direction of the incoming fire. When the explosion erupted, screams sounded from the jungle.

Jake and Hank leaped up and sprayed more bullets into the attack, then sprinted back toward the village using the denseness of the close-packed trees as cover. Pieces of bark splattered around them and leaves were clipped from branches in the furious fire sent after their fleeing forms.

Time was not being wasted back in the village. Although there had been no opportunity to prepare permanent firing positions, Falconi had set up a perimeter with temporary fighting holes similar to the ones the advance guards like Jake Bernstein and Hank Valverde used out in the woods. The other pair of outlying pickets, Kim and Calvin Culpepper from Alpha Fire Team, had also withdrawn per standard operational procedure when the dawn assault first erupted.

The attackers pressed in closer now, their flying bullets ripping through the huts of the villagers. Cries and screams from the peasants gave pitiful evidence the civilians were sustaining casualties.

Falconi got onto the Prick Six. "Team leaders. The villagers are gonna get slaughtered if we don't haul ass. We'll break toward the south. Alphas go first."

Chris Hawkins shouted concise orders. Kim's M79 grenade launcher barked three times, the forty-millimeter projectiles blowing an opening in the jungle wall. The Aussie, Bill Taylor, went to the left, Calvin Culpepper to the right and Chris followed Kim straight up the middle.

That side of the jungle exploded as a heavy machine gun pounded the edge of the village. The Alphas, reeling back under the onslaught, were forced to return to their original positions.

"Falcon," Chris panted into the Prick-Six, "we're catching hell on the south. We couldn't break through."

Falconi wasted no time in contacting Top Gordon. "Top, clear us a path through the west."

"Roger, Falcon!"

Blue Richards, shrieking the Rebel yell, went straight down the middle like an NFL running back. His M16 spit fire. Top and Hank covered the left flank while Malpractice and Jake took the right. But the incoming fusillades on that side roared up, making the Bravo Fire Team attack falter, then come to a grudging halt.

Top wasn't discouraged. "Push on, goddamnit!"

140

The Bravos made another attempt, gaining a few meters until their progress was again halted by superior firepower. Top, shoving a fresh magazine into his weapon, saw that disaster was only a matter of moments away. "Pull back!"

Hank Valverde performed his grenadier chores admirably, blowing away three eager Algerians with one round. Then he rushed back with the others.

Falconi ordered the men into a tighter perimeter. The outer huts of the village were burning now, and several dead civilians lay sprawled around them. The rest of the population had instinctively moved inward, getting in the Black Eagles' midst, causing considerable confusion and muddling around.

Blue Richards, situated behind the well, tried several times to get off a few rounds, but the peasants were spoiling his field of fire. He glanced back at Master Sgt. Top Gordon. "We got to haul ass! These folks is a-spoilin' my aim!"

Top waved over at him. "We working on it, Blue, believe me!" He finally got a clear shot between a couple of huts. Not wanted to let the opportunity go by, he hosed several long bursts in that direction. He saw an Algerian, with a bloody, mangled chest, stumble out of the jungle in shock, then collapse at the hamlet's edge.

The team leader gritted his teeth in grim satisfaction and swung the M16 for another salvo, but Falconi's voice again sounded over the Prick-Six. "Bravo! Bravo! Lead us out east."

Top raised his own radio to his mouth. "Roger, Falcon." He yelled to his team, "Hank! To the east. Let's go, guys. Blue, stick with me!"

Hank let off several rounds in the direction of their attackers while going at a dead run. Top and Blue covered his left. Malpractice and Jake did the honors on the right side. They hit dead-on with a squad of Alger-

141

ian riflemen. Hank, not having time to reload the M79, used it as a club when the two groups collided. He swung hard against the head of the lead Red, smashing him to the ground.

Malpractice and Blue shot away a trio of eager enemy riflemen coming out of the woods. Top and Jake Bernstein got into a good position and riddled several more pushy Algerians.

But there were more behind them—plenty more.

"They're outflanking us!" Hank yelled. He managed to alleviate the problem temporarily with a couple of well-placed grenades that sent a pair of the sneakier types cartwheeling through the air.

Top saw that the vacancy was about to the refilled—along with more in front. "Break contact! Move to the rear!"

Back in the village, Falconi and the Alphas had their hands full with attacks on the other side. When the major saw Top and his men stumbling back into the village while covering each other with superbly coordinated rear-guard shooting, he knew his men couldn't get out in that direction either.

Chief Brewster was in a particularly bad mood. Refusing to let his valuable PRC-77 radio get lost, he had the double trouble of dragging the commo gear from firing position to firing position while raking the attackers with bursts from his M16. His brawny arm muscles were knotted and cramped with the effort, and the expression on his face betrayed his fury. "C'mon and die for it, motherfuckers!" he bellowed.

A lone Algerian made a dash from the jungle toward the cover of a burning hut. The chief, using one arm, swung the muzzle and gave the Red a bit of lead like he would have a flying duck back in Iowa. Three pulls on the trigger, though a bit jerky, did the job as two of the rounds dumped the man to the ground.

Ray Swift Elk, ever the warrior and scout, had managed to use the smoke from the burning huts much like his ancestors would use a prairie fire. He kept the billowing clouds between himself and the enemy, then found an opening that led out of the village into the surrounding jungle.

Quickly slashing through the dense brush, he dove to the ground. With the noise of the firing to cover any sound, Swift Elk was able to move faster than under normal circumstances. Within a few moments the Sioux was behind the attackers.

The depth of the Algerian formation was shallow, and he was able to see the village while observing them. Swift Elk caught occasional sightings of the other Black Eagles through the drifting smoke in the hamlet. He could also see the mounting casualties among the villagers. A plan quickly formed in his sharp mind. He grasped the Prick-Six. "Falcon, this is the scout. Over."

"Roger, Scout," came the reply.

"I'm on the other side of the bad guys on the west side of the village. I can clear a path out to the jungle for you with some artistic backshooting on my part. Over."

Falconi's voice was loud and clear. "Sounds like we got 'em surrounded. Over."

Swift Elk laughed. "Roger that, baby! Give me ten seconds to start my doo-dah on this side, then come on out. Over."

"Roger, wilco. Go for it! Out!" Falconi said. He didn't have time to explain the situation, but with the Black Eagles, it wouldn't be necessary. At the end of a ten-count, he shouted his orders to the detachment that was now drawn in close. "Top, lead us to the west. Chris, you and the Alphas follow with me. Go! Go! Go!"

The Bravo Fire Team again formed their "V" formation with Hank Valverde at the head. When the detachment focused all their firing power on that side, it caught the Algerians by surprise.

Then Swift Elk's weapon hit them from the rear, causing a momentary hesitation on their part. Some turned to face the new threat, others decided to slug it out to the front. It was an uncoordinated and weak effort — it was also fatal.

The front troops toward the village caught the full brunt of the initial Black Eagle bursts. Grenades from both Kim's and Hank's M79s blew gaps in their ranks, and the M16 fire swept the others away. The men in the rear, confused by the casualties they sustained from Swift Elk's sweeps of automatic fire, turned toward that source of hell, then caught the full brunt of the main attack.

Falconi, catching up with Top, passed both the master sergeant and Hank Valverde, running until Swift Elk came out from his cover and signaled to him. The Sioux tried to see past his commanding officer at the detachment. "Did everybody make it?" he asked breathlessly.

"So far, so good," Falconi replied. "But the bastards on the other side of the village will be here as quick as they figure we're gone."

Top Gordon caught up with him. "Damn! You run fast, don't you?"

"I'm a little excited, I guess," Falconi said. "Form your team here, Top. Hold 'em up long enough to slow the sons of bitches, then withdraw through the Alphas. Then they'll do the same after you've re-established yourself farther back."

"Yes, sir!" Top signaled to his crew and formed them up. This time, instead of being at the front, Hank Valverde and his grenade launcher were situated at the back to act as a mini-artillery battery.

The Mexican-American arranged his ammo load for the next phase of fighting. He noted the Alphas moving back to situate themselves. He took advantage of the lull to take a drink from his canteen. "Looks like we're going into a rear-guard action, Top."

"It's the only way we can break contact," Top said.

Malpractice McCorckel, quickly digging in nearby, was more to the point. "It's the only way we can survive."

The Algerians moved slowly and cautiously through the dense smoke that hung low in the Tinh-Ly-Nho. Maj. Omar Ahmar, his AK47 at the ready, walked slowly behind the first three skirmish lines that led the unit into the village.

The Red officer noted the dead scattered among the huts. In a way it reminded him of the Algerian War against the French when an unlucky cluster of stone hovels would be caught in the middle of ferocious clashes of rebels and paras. He looked in vain for a dead Black Eagle, but could see none.

Suddenly a lone villager stepped out from between the huts. He held a beautiful, but very dead woman in his arms. He screamed at the Algerian major in Vietnamese, his rage and grief apparent in the tone of misery in his voice.

Ahmar could not understand a word the man said. Nor did he know that this was Ngwan, the VC collaborator. The Algerian, pissed off, said nothing. He swung his AK47 around and blasted the Red away, blowing both him and the woman through the burning straw of the nearest hut.

Then the fighting started again.

A sudden build-up of automatic weapon salvos peaked, but quickly died off. After a few moments it began again, then once more faded away.

Ahmar rushed forward and found the leader of his advance platoon slowly moving his men forward. The young lieutenant, his face streaked with smoke, smudge and sweat, was near exhaustion in the steamy heat. His voice was cracked with the strain. "The *banduk* are now fighting and running—fighting and running."

Ahmar, the veteran, knew exactly what was going on. He'd used such tactics many times himself. "They are leapfrogging to the rear," he explained. "It is a rear-guard action designed to delay us. Eventually, they hope to break clear and escape from our attack."

The lieutenant's face was scarlet with shame. "*Hazin ana*," he apologized, "I fear they will succeed."

Ahmar listened to another build-up and recession of fire before he spoke again. "It would be extremely difficult to stop them in this dense forest."

The young officer was chagrined. "Then will they escape us?"

Ahmar surprised the other Algerian by calmly smiling. "They will break contact with us, yes. But there is something else waiting for them out in that jungle."

"*Sahih*—is that true?"

"Of course, comrade lieutenant," Ahmar assured him with confidence. "This entire battle has been well-planned. The fighting is going as expected, and Phase Two will begin shortly."

# Chapter 14

Archie Dobbs did a series of sit-ups on the bed, then swung his legs over the side and closed his eyes.

The soldier in the bunk next to him watched carefully. "Feel any dizziness, Archie?"

Archie took a deep breath. "Not too bad this time. How does my face look?"

The other man, a heavily bandaged sergeant from the 101st Airborne named Davis, leaned across the space between their beds and looked carefully at his companion. "Hey, not too bad. Really. How're you feeling?"

"A hell of a lot better," Archie said. He slid to the floor and took a few steps. He smiled almost wickedly. "Great! That's how I feel."

Davis looked down toward the ward office. "Nurse Pembelton oughta be leaving for the staff meeting pretty quick."

Archie got back on the bed. "Right. When she goes, I make my move, man."

"How're you gonna get out of Long Binh?" Davis asked. "Even if you get your uniform, you can't just walk around wherever you please without a pass."

"I'll hitch a ride in a truck that's got a work detail in it," Archie said. "If I sit in with a bunch o' guys, the MPs on the gate won't ask nothing."

"Yeah," Davis conceded. "It'll prob'ly work." He leaned forward and looked back down toward the end of the ward again. "Hey, Archie. She's hattin' up, man."

Archie, now allowed by the doctor to walk around his bed as long as he held on tightly and moved slowly, nonchalantly got to his feet. He shuffled his feet and purposely made himself appear to be weak and unsteady.

Davis laughed. "If she sees you, man, she won't figger you're goin' no place." He winked. "And I don't think that nurse wants you to go, Archie. She really digs you."

Archie grinned. "Yeah. I know." He assumed a tired, sad expression on his face and glanced down at the office. He immediately brightened. "She's gone, baby — and that means me too!"

"Good luck," Davis said sincerely.

Archie walked slowly, but steadily, between the row of beds until he reached the front of the ward. Then he turned to the door opposite the office and opened it. There was a long rack along one side of the room. Various uniforms, mostly fatigues, all belonging to the patients, hung there under tags that bore large letters of the alphabet. Archie went down past the A's, B's and C's until he reached the D's. He found a set of fatigues belonging to him on the other side of his new buddy Davis' clothes. The uniform, along with the boots sitting underneath it, had been brought in from Peterson Field by Fagin. There was also a paper bag holding underwear and socks. These items were meant to be used in case the chickenshit Doctor Davenport relented and granted him a pass to leave the ward for a few hours. Archie's immediate plans involved a far more permanent departure.

He slipped out of the blue issue pajamas and reached in the sack for his underwear. Archie dressed quickly, suffering his only bout of dizziness when he bent over too fast to lace up his boots. Finally, fully and properly dressed, complete with Black Eagle beret, he squared his shoulders and walked toward the door.

The flimsy portal swung open and Nurse Pembelton stood there pouting, her hands on her hips. "Dobbs!"

Archie smiled. "Call me Archie."

"The first thing I did when I came back was to look down at your bed," Nurse Pembelton said. "When I saw you'd gone and read that silly expression on Davis' face I knew exactly what was going on."

"What's your name—I mean your first name?" Archie asked sweetly.

"Betty Lou," she answered. "And don't change the subject. Are you trying to get me in trouble?"

"Oh, no, Betty Lou," Archie said, easing toward her. "You must know by now how I feel about you."

Her voice faltered. "N-now, now. I don't know any such thing."

Archie closed in on her, putting his face close to hers. "I'm wild about you, Betty Lou."

She nervously wet her lips. "See here, now. You're—you're an enlisted man and I'm an officer."

He slipped his arms around her waist. "Sweetheart, you're the best-looking lieutenant I've seen in seven years in this here army."

"Stop that!"

Archie kissed her tenderly, then with more pressure.

Betty Lou Pembelton pushed him away—a little bit, but not quite enough to make him let go. "This is not proper—Archie."

"How can you deny the feelings we have for each other, Betty Lou? I know you dig me. And you can see how I feel about you too, right?"

"Let's just wait and see how this relationship—"

Archie interrupted her. "Give in to your heart! To your emotions!"

She wavered, then seemed to melt in his arms. "Oh,

yes, Archie! Oh, dear, sweet Archie!" She allowed him to kiss her again. She clung to him then suddenly became angry and pushed the Black Eagle away. "You can't fool me! You're just being nice so I'll let you leave. Well, I won't!" She freed herself and rushed to the door. "Get back into those pajamas and down to your bed — or I'll report you!" She went back on the ward.

Archie watched her leave. He was tempted to bolt for freedom, but he knew she would alert the MP detachment and it would only be a matter of time before he would be back in the hospital — this time in the stockade ward. He slowly changed back into the pajamas and went back out onto the ward. Archie stopped by the office. "Thank you."

Betty Lou Pembelton looked at him. "For what?"

"You could have turned me in," Archie said. "But you gave me a break." He noticed she'd been crying a little.

"Please — please, go back to your bed."

"Sure, Betty Lou." Archie walked a few steps, then turned and came back. "It ain't true what you said."

"What are you talking about?" she asked.

"I really do like you," Archie said. "I wasn't being that way 'cause I wanted you to let me haul ass."

"Please — return to your bed."

"Sure." Archie walked down the row of patients and got back between the sheets.

Davis sadly shook his head. "The bitch caught you, huh?"

Archie snapped a furious look at the other soldier. "Say that again, Davis, and as soon as you're outta this dump I'll break your fuckin nose!"

"Jesus Christ!" Davis said angrily. "You're real touchy all of a sudden, ain't you?"

* * *

Blue Richards, bringing up the rear of the Bravos, pounded down the jungle trail. "They's on my ass!" he announced to the Alphas as he passed them and continued to the spot Top Gordon had chosen to place the Bravos' temporary defensive line.

Calvin Culpepper and Bill Taylor, their M16s ready, only had to wait a moment before the first Algerians appeared in pursuit. They pumped their M16 triggers, spraying the unfortunate men in the forefront with deadly, automatic bursts of flying slugs.

These men dropped in a heap, one rolling over before dying. Their comrades behind them threw themselves to the ground and returned the fire.

Kim, his faithful M79 barking like a mad Korean dog, added his own special brand of firepower while Chris Hawkins did the same.

More Algerians came, pressing forward, until the pressure of return fire was too much. Chris could hear them crashing through the trees on both sides in an attempt to pull a flanking maneuver. He gave the orders to withdraw, and the Alphas backed up a few steps still firing, then turned and ran like hell down the trail. They kept going until they reached Maj. Robert Falconi, Chief Brewster and Ray Swift Elk. The Alphas only waved as they past the Command Element. Next they ran through the Bravos' position. Only then did they stop and situate themselves once again.

This time it was the Command Element that withstood the hit. Three M16s sent out a cone-shaped volley that swept through the Algerians pressing in on the fire team. The North Africans wavered, then again stopped and returned the fusillade in an attempt to blow the defenders away.

But, within a few moments, Falconi, the chief and Swift Elk were running like hell after delaying the enemy advance and knocking off a couple of them.

The deadly routine of leapfrog continued for another two hours. It was obvious the game was over after the Alphas, once again withdrawing to leave the Command Element in the vanguard, headed back toward the rear.

Falconi and Swift Elk each took one side of the trail, while Chief Brewster, hampered as always by his radio gear, was back toward the rear where he could have a head start in the withdrawal.

The jungle was eerily quiet. Not even the animals made sounds in the vacuum left by the sudden absence of blasting weaponry.

Falconi wiped at the seat stinging his eyes, waiting like a tensed tiger for the expected assault.

The stillness continued.

Swift Elk looked over at the detachment commander and shrugged in a quizzical manner. Then he pointed to himself, then down the trail to ask if he should make a reconnaissance.

Falconi nodded affirmatively, then watched the Sioux Indian move out to do his dangerous job of scout.

Falconi took the opportunity offered by the lull in the fighting to treat himself to a long drink of the luke-warm water in his canteen. Chief Brewster, unable to free himself from the extra weight of the PRC-77 radio, did likewise. The sailor caught his commander's eye and winked. "Exciting afternoon, huh, Skipper?" he whispered.

Falconi winked back. "Yeah. It should be the talk of this year's social season." He brought the Prick-Six to his ear. "Alpha. This is Falcon. How're you guys doing? Over."

Chris Hawkins' voice, the New England accent deep and resonant, came back over the receiver. "Hanging tight, Falcon. Out."

Falconi could picture the team, with Kim eagerly shoving the muzzle of his grenade launcher toward the enemy, tensed for action. He checked in on Top's guys. "Bravo. This is Falcon. What's your status? Over."

"We're getting dry, Falcon," Top Gordon replied over his own radio. "Aside from that, we're numbah-fucking-one. Out."

Falconi checked his own canteens again. Top Gordon had brought up an important point that had been overlooked during the pressing combat of the previous few hours. Water was going to be a problem unless they could get to a creek or river quick. The weather of Southeast Asia was very unforgiving of individuals who risked dehydration. Heavy sweating not only sapped strength, it removed vital fluids needed to stay alive and healthy.

A rustling ahead caught Falconi's attention, but he relaxed when he noted Ray Swift Elk approaching him. "What're those bastards doing, Ray?" he said.

"They broke contact, sir," Swift Elk replied. "I came across about four bodies before I turned back."

"They were truly catching hell," Falconi said, not without a hint of respect in his voice, "but the sons of bitches still pressed on."

"This thick jungle couldn't've been better for us," Swift Elk said. "What's our next move?"

"The first thing is water," Falconi said, pulling a map from his large side pocket. He spread it out and studied the terrain features represented by the various symbols. He noted a thin blue line. "Here we go. Looks like a small creek."

Swift Elk checked the location. "It ain't far. We can make it in about an hour."

"Let's go then," Falconi said. He once again used the Prick-Six to raise the fire teams, and set up the column for movement. "After we refill these canteens we'll give

153

some thought to a few more pressing matters."

"Yeah," Swift Elk said. "Like a re-supply drop. I need some bullets."

Falconi motioned to Chief Brewster. "Give me the PRC-77. I'll spell you a bit."

The chief sighed. "Jesus, Skipper. Thanks a hell of a lot. My shoulders are beginning to think they're lugging a goddamned anchor complete with chain."

Swift Elk moved up to the head of the column with Falconi and the chief following. The detachment, with the Bravos covering the rear, began the slow torturous process of moving through the monsoon forest.

Under normal conditions, where noise discipline would not have been necessary, such movement would have been difficult and exhausting. But the Black Eagles had to travel as silent as possible, yet still break trail. It was tougher yet on Ray Swift Elk. He was not only in the lead, but had to retrace his steps from time to time to avoid losing contact with the men he was scouting for.

They had been moving for half an hour when the ambush hit them from the right side. It was a sudden, unexpected explosion of AK47 fire. Malpractice McCorckel and Hank Valverde were the first to catch sight of the bushwhackers.

"Viet Cong!" Hank yelled instinctively as he hosed back in the direction of the incoming 7.62-millimeter rounds.

The other Black Eagles, following standard procedure, also returned fire while breaking into a fast run to clear the area. Noise discipline was no longer something to be considered.

This attack was behind Ray Swift Elk. He stopped and waited to cover his buddies when they came storming toward him. He didn't have long to tarry before Chief Brewster and Falconi made an appearance. Those two joined him and added their own volume of bullets to his bursts until both the Alphas and Bravos had made it through the storm of steel.

The shooting suddenly stopped.

"What the hell was that all about?" Chris Hawkins asked.

"I think we stumbled onto a VC patrol," Falconi surmised.

Blue Richards shifted his rucksack. "Let's go back and get them sumbitches. Whatcha say, Skipper?"

Before Falconi could answer, the entire jungle around them erupted into a large volume of fire. Ricochets zinged off tree trunks and passing bullets slapped through the air and sliced into the brush and lower branches.

Top Gordon summed up the situation in one short sentence. "Those fuckers are in cahoots with them Algerians."

Chris Hawkins was a bit more precise. "We've been set up. Here we go again!"

"Again, hell!" Falconi said. "This is part of the same battle. We just thought we'd broken contact."

The detachment formed into a hasty perimeter as the first of the attacking enemy riflemen moved in on them.

# Chapter 15

The shrieking Viet Cong burst through the brush and leaped into the Black Eagles' positions.

Bill Taylor and Calvin Culpepper met the assault head-on. Each only had time for quick firebursts that dumped the lead attackers before others behind literally collided with them. Luckily for the two Black Eagles, both men were big and brawny. Calvin backhanded one Charlie so hard that the small man stumbled sideways and blocked the progress of another Red.

Taylor, an experienced pub-brawler, battered away with his M16 rifle in his left hand while the right pumped punches at two more Viet Cong closing in on him.

Despite these initial successes, however, the pressing mob built up around them. Chris Hawkins and Chun Kim, coming in from opposite sides, took off the pressure with salvos of bullets fired quickly from the hip. Calvin and Taylor both backed off enough to be able to once again bring their weapons to bear.

"Pull back!" Chris ordered.

The four Alphas formed into a skirmish line and covered their own retreat deeper back into the trees. They kept going until they joined Falconi, Swift Elk and the chief. A minute later Master Sgt. Top Gordon's Bravo Team came in from the other side.

Falconi was now alarmed at the tight formation the detachment had been forced into. The young Algerian lieutenant back at the landing zone had paid with his entire platoon while in a similar situation. They were packed into such a dense mob that the major could shout to his team leaders without using the radio.

"Spread it out! If they bring in MGs or mortars, we've had it!" He pointed to Top and indicated which direction he wanted the Bravos to go.

Top Gordon bellowed his own orders, and his team surged forward under the covering explosions of Hank Valverde's grenades. The effort paid off as the VC, not expecting such an action to break the momentum of their pressing assault, sustained a sudden influx of heavy casualties that left a gap in their formation. Gordon's guys filled in the vacuum, then found more opportunity to press on when the Reds gave way some more under the murderous mixed semi- and full-automatic M16 fire that swept back and forth across the small battle front.

Top was about to congratulate himself when a quick glance off to one side gave him a sight that chilled him down to the core of his soldier's soul.

It was Malpractice McCorckel who verbalized the situation. "Those fucking Algerians are back!"

The unmistakable tan uniforms were clearly visible in a group that now appeared in the midst of the black pajamas of the Charlies. Top, now free of any enemy to his front, turned his team to hit this new threat. But a sudden influx of more VC forced him to continue away from the scene of the fight.

At this same time, Falconi and the Alphas were pushed in the opposite direction. They made several probes under the major's direction, but each effort was thwarted as more and more of the enemy appeared around them.

Within the space of a few moments, the Black Eagle Detachment was split. The Command Element and Alpha Fire Team were in one group, and Top's Bravos were in another. They were effectively cut off from each other.

There was no choice for the Command Element and the Alphas but to once again form a perimeter. Chun Kim, an experienced combat veteran, quickly recognized how important his beloved M79 had become. He left the tightening outer formation and moved toward the center where he could fire projectiles in any necessary direction.

Now the incoming rounds were joined by heavy machine gunfire, and the whole world seemed to turn to one endless roar of gunnery. The Black Eagles of the Command Element and Alpha Team hugged the ground and returned fire until the tropical night began to quickly darken the murderous jungle.

Even then, the Communist firing continued hot and heavy.

The heavy breathing of sleeping men filled the ward. Now and then one of the wounded would groan a bit in his sleep, but other than that, it was relatively quiet.

Archie Dobbs could see the weak light coming from the office down at the other end. He checked the luminous dial on his watch and noticed it was almost two a.m. — and he knew which nurse had caught duty that night.

He slipped from his bed and put on the white slippers he'd been issued as a patient. Making sure he made no disturbance, the Black Eagle walked slowly to the head of the ward. When he arrived at the office, he tapped softly on the door.

Lt. Betty Lou Pembelton looked up from her *Cosmo-*

*politan*. She looked at Archie with a suspicious glare, but the expression on her face softened within a couple of moments. The nurse regained her composure. "What do you want, Arch—er, Dobbs?"

Archie entered the office and sat down on the chair beside hers. "I got to talk to you, Betty Lou."

"I'm not letting you off the ward," she said, scooting a couple of feet away. "So you can just forget that!"

"I ain't thinking about going away now," Archie protested gently. "In fact, that's the last thing I want to do. It's just that I got to be with you, baby."

"Don't call me baby."

"OK. Can I call you darling?"

"No! You can call me ma'am or lieutenant!" Betty Lou snapped under her breath.

Archie leaned forward and kissed her lightly on the mouth. He smiled. "Can I call you sweetheart?"

"No!"

"How about dear? Pet? Snookums?"

Betty Lou's clamp on her emotions gave way. She laughed. "Archie, stop it."

This time he took her in his arms and pulled her close, forcing her to rise with him until they were both standing. Then he kissed her mouth with a gentle pressure, tightening his embrace.

Betty Lou moaned softly, then finally gave in and put her arms around his neck. She stood on her tiptoes and kissed him back. Finally, she gently broke off the contact. "Oh, Archie! What am I going to do with you?"

"I don't know, Lieutenant."

"Call me darling," Betty Lou said.

Archie grinned and kissed her again. This time he brought his tongue into it. The woman pressed her body close to his, feeling him grow firm under the GI pajamas. This time they clung together longer as the

159

Black Eagle let his hands drop to her buttocks, kneading them softly.

"I want you, Betty Lou."

Her eyes gave silent consent.

Archie, gentle with a woman for the first time in his life, took her hand and led her out of the ward office to the storeroom on the other side of the narrow corridor. He pushed the door shut after they went inside, locking the latch. He said it again, "I want you, Betty Lou."

These were two healthy young people in a war situation where there was no time for the courting etiquette demanded by society. They both silently disrobed in the dim light cast by the forty-watt bulb overhead.

Archie kissed Betty Lou again, then led her to the mattresses stored along the far wall of the room. He only paused long enough to let his gaze devour the sight of those beautiful breasts that he'd only been able to imagine before.


Malpractice McCorckel, moving slowly in the dark, pushed his canteen under the water of the creek. There was a slight gurgling noise as it filled. He turned his eyes toward the site where the Command Element and Alphas were cut off from them. The fighting in that area had been silent for more than three quarters of an hour. "I wish to God I knew for sure what was going on over there."

Besides him, almost completely invisible in the jungle night, Blue Richards took a long drink of the cool water. "I don't like all that quiet. It's enough to give a feller the willies."

"It doesn't mean anything," Hank Valverde said. "It's too damned dark for any real combat, Both sides are probably laying low."

"Anyhow, I'll bet the Falcon and the others'd like some o' this water, huh?" Blue said.

Top Gordon, his own thirst slaked now, nodded. "They'll get their chance tomorrow."

There was a muffled yawn as the Marine, Jake Bernstein, settled himself into a more comfortable position. He came quickly to the point. "We're gonna have to go in there and get 'em out, aren't we, Top?"

A sudden fusillade broke out and continued unabated for a full ten minutes. Then it broke off.

"Things ain't so quite out there after all," Malpractice McCorckel remarked.

Blue Richards was in a sad mood. "First ol' Archie gets medevaced, then the Falcon and the Alphas get cut off." He sighed aloud. "Damn! I feel like my favorite herd o' pigs has been split up."

Top looked his way in the dark. "You're real elegant, Blue."

"Wal," Blue said, "I hate to be so damn sentimental, but that's the way I'm a-feelin'."

Hank Valverde, the supply sergeant, had other things on his mind. "We're running short on goods. If we don't get an airdrop in, this whole damn shooting match is headed for hell."

"The first thing on the agenda is getting back with the rest of the detachment," Top said.

"Hell, Top," Malpractice said. "We'll be going for broke in the morning, won't we?"

"There's a well-used cliche that sums up the situation exactly," Top said. "Do or die."


Archie and Betty Lou had dressed. They sat together on the same mattress where they'd made love, and shared a cigarette while leaning against the wall.

Archie had a chance to tell Betty Lou all about the

Black Eagles. He covered everyone, telling of Falconi's leadership, Top's dignified example he set for everyone, Malpractice's mothering, Kim's craziness with his grenade launcher and Calvin Culpepper's artistry with explosives. Not being a particularly modest person, he didn't gloss over a bit on his own talents as a scout, but he allowed that Ray Swift Elk was probably the only man in the world who could come close to his own accomplishments in tracking and acting as point man.

Then he told her about the detachment as a unit, expounding on the basic philosophy of following the Latin motto of *calcitra clunis* — kick ass — but adding the camaraderie and dependability of each man.

Betty Lou learned what being a Black Eagle really meant. And she fully understood for the first time how important it was to her lover to give his all for Major Falconi and the others.

"You really love those guys, don't you?" Betty Lou asked.

Archie finished the cigarette and pressed it out on the floor. He condensed his feelings in one flat statement that he spoke with the deepest and most genuine of sincerity. "I'd die for 'em."

"Yes," Betty Lou said. "I believe you would. And they would do the same for you — and each other, too."

"Yeah."

Betty Lou kissed him on the mouth, then stood up. "I'd better get back to the ward office."

Archie got to his feet. "I'll head for my bed before any of the guys wake up."

She slipped her arms around him, and held up her face for another kiss. After he'd pressed his lips on hers, Betty Lou stepped back. "I'll see you later."

"Yeah. At morning doctor's rounds."

"No, Archie. I mean later." She pointed to his uniform on the hanger as she checked her watch. "Put

162

it on. You'll have a good three-hour lead before they find—" she laughed—"that is, until *I* find you missing."

Archie grabbed her and kissed her hard, then pulled the fatigues off the rack.

Lt. Col. Gregori Krashchenko, unable to sleep as always, sat at the open window of his room and smoked one cigarette after another. His dark thoughts, which carried pictures of a KGB firing squad, were interrupted by a knock on his door. Irritated, he turned toward the distraction.

"*Da?*" he said, speaking Russian. He didn't give a damn if the nocturnal visitor could understand him or not.

The door opened and a young NVA soldier stepped in. He spoke a halting brand of French, but could be understood. "*Monsieur le Major* Truong want for you to see you in the room of the radio."

"Very well," Krashchenko said. Then he added sarcastically, "I shall go to see *Monsieur le Major* in 'the room of the radio.' " He lit another cigarette off the one nearly finished and strode after the soldier.

Krashchenko's thoughts turned blacker as he walked down the corridor. There was bad news for him, no doubt, and that yellow, slant-eyed bastard Truong couldn't wait to give it to him.

When they arrived at the communications room, the young NVA trooper opened the door and stood respectfully at attention. Krashchenko, putting on a bold front, walked in like he was at a formal parade of a guards' tank division. "What is it, Truong?"

Truong, smoking his own brand of cigarettes, looked up from where he stood by the radio speaker. "Some news that will be of interest to you, Krashchenko."

"Well?"

163

Truong took a drag off his smoke. "The Black Eagle detachment has been cut in half. One group is completely surrounded and isolated."

Krashchenko's mouth hung open. "Is it true?"

"Of course," Truong said unemotionally. "And Major Ahmar has assured us that the trapped unit will be destroyed or captured within an hour of today's dawn." He paused. "Do you call that good news?"

Loud laughter broke from the Russian KGB officer. "Not for Major Robert Falconi!"

# Chapter 16

Dawn was brand new and dully glowing as Blue Richards moved slowly through the brush. He used the same caution he'd employ if he was coon hunting back in Alabama. But this time there were no hunting dogs sniffing out the game. Instead, it was his own senses — raw and alert — that he had to rely on as he led the Bravo Fire Team toward the sound of the firing that had been building up since first light.

Top Gordon could barely see the ass-end of Blue's tiger-striped camouflaged fatigue uniform as he followed at the ready. Jake Bernstein was on the right flank and Malpractice McCorckel covered the left side of their formation. Hank Valverde, the M79 grenade launcher locked and loaded, brought up the rear, ready to cover any situation with his dwindling supply of explosive projectiles.

Top Gordon's plan was simple and to the point. The previous evening's fighting, combined with the bursts of fire that had heralded the new day's beginning, gave stark evidence that the Command Element and Alpha Fire Team were unable to break out of the ring of Reds that surrounded them. The master sergeant figured the best thing to do was to penetrate into the interior and link up with Falconi, Chris Hawkins and the others. Then, with everyone joined together again, crash back out through the side of the line weakened by the Bravos' violent entrance.

But Blue had yet to make contact with any of the enemy soldiers as he continued to lead the team into the combat zone. The shooting, which had been building up and dying down, finally steadied a bit. Then the crescendo of blasting weapons gradually built up until the jungle rocked under the concussion of a violent battle.

A couple of minutes later, Blue came eyeball to eyeball with the Algerians.

The Alabaman's M16 spit out in sweeps of automatic fire. The flankers, Malpractice and Jake Bernstein, kicked off a steady rate of semiauto firing. At that particular time they had not caught sight of the enemy, but obviously the unseen sons of bitches were out there to the front somewhere.

"Hit 'em!" Top yelled.

Hank Valverde blasted away with the M79. When the first grenade exploded in the brush ahead, the Bravos charged.

An Algerian with a Russian RPD light machine gun tried to whip his weapon around to meet this attack from the rear, but he went down, screaming under the flying slugs of the Black Eagles. Likewise, the two riflemen assigned to cover him died in the fusillades that swept their position.

Blue led his team in a dead run and jumped over the three dead men. Top was hot on his heels, unable to lend much fire support for fear of hitting his point and flank men. But Blue, Malpractice and Jake kept up their deadly bursts of 5.56-millimeter rounds while Hank Valverde cleared the area ahead as best he could with the grenades.

Now the enemy formation was denser and more numerous. The surprised Algerians responded with increased return fire. Blue, the air around him thick with flying bullets, instinctively ducked his head as he pushed on to the growing hellish resistance. Malpractice and Jake were forced in closer to him while Hank caught up and nearly collided with Top Gordon.

Then the hand-to-hand began.

Surprisingly, it wasn't Blue that hit head-on first. Instead it was Malpractice McCorckel, and he had to make a hard half-left in from the direction he was running. His opponent was a tall, husky Algerian sergeant. The man whose squad was aligned as skirmishers to his front, forgot all about his small command as he turned to face Malpractice's yelling assault.

The North African was an old hand and knew what he was doing. He swung his Kalashnikov and blocked Malpractice's bayonet thrust. A skillful follow through with a horizontal butt-stroke would have put out the Black Eagle's lights, but Malpractice ducked under the attack and came up with the heel of his hand. He struck under the man's chin, snapping his head back.

The Algerian, though dazed and suffering from an instant case of double vision from the punch, brought the AK47 around for another swing from the opposite direction. But before he could complete the maneuver, Malpractice stomped the guy's instep with every ounce of weight he could muster.

The bones of the foot gave way and the Algerian screamed in raging pain. Now it was Malpractice's turn to use his weapon, and he slammed it hard — once! twice! — into the guy's skull.

It was the Algerian's lights that went out.

Blue Richards, at that same time, finally made physical contact. A wild-eyed young North African stood his ground in the classic "*en garde*" position, holding his AK47 at high port. Blue was not impressed. He kept the affair short and sweet. The Black

Eagle stepped up his run to close the distance between himself and the Red, then climaxed his charge with a bayonet to the throat. The Navy Seal withdrew it and rammed it home again. This time it was in the belly. The Algerian dropped his weapon. He went into deep shock, barely managing to limp off to one side before falling to the ground and rolling over in grimacing agony.

Blue, with Top now bellowing behind him, let the wounded man go. He charged forward again, automatic sprays of bullets clearing the way ahead.

Suddenly the Algerians melted away to the front. The Bravos swept through the rear of the enemy perimeter and crashed into the shot-away brush where Falconi and the others were in a desperate defense posture.

Ray Swift Elk quickly directed the Bravos—with the exception of Top Gordon—into firing positions to fill gaps in the thin line.

Top protested the move to Falconi. "Hey, Skipper! Get the guys up and moving. We'll get the hell out the same damn way we came in here."

Falconi shook his head. "You got in here, Top, because those bastards let you in. They're wrapped around us tighter'n a number-eight jumpboot on a number-ten foot."

Chris Hawkins joined them from his side of the position. The news he brought was grim. "They filled in the gap the Bravos came through," he announced. "We're sewed up once more."

Tom pulled his full canteens from his belt and tossed them over. "What the hell! We just showed up to buy the drinks anyhow." He started to yell orders to the other Bravos to pass around their water, but could see it was already being done.

Then the surrounding jungle exploded, sending

salvos of full automatic fire to rake the Black Eagles.

Falconi and Top hit the dirt together. Falconi handed the canteen back. "The water was delicious, Top. But as thirsty as I am, I wished you'd've brought ammo instead."

Chuck Fagin put the telephone back on its cradle. "Commo rooms says no contact."

His companion in the office on the first floor of SOG Headquarters was a blond Army warrant officer who sported short-cropped hair and a huge handlebar moustache. The man, who looked like he belonged on a Viking longship, took a drink from the beer can in his hand. "If I could get my chopper in close enough, we'd be within radio range of that PRC-77 they have. Hell, we could even raise 'em on a Prick-Six if that was what we had to use."

"I thought of that," Fagin said. "All yesterday I've been bugging hell out of G3 to clear some flights, but they won't take a chance because I can't pinpoint Falconi's exact location. Those guys want the grid coordinates right down to ten digits."

The warrant officer drained the can and tossed it over into a nearby wastebasket. "Yeah. They're real assholes about wild goose chases."

Fagin leaned back in his chair. "Goddamnit! They sent the guys into a situation where they were outnumbered to begin with. You'd think the brass would be willing to bend the rules in a case like this."

The warrant officer walked over to the small refrigerator and fetched them both fresh beers. He'd just handed Fagin his when the office intercom buzzed.

"Yeah?" Fagin asked irritably.

The voice on the other end was that of an MP guard. "I got a guy down here at the entrance without credentials, Mister Fagin. But he's got the proper password. Says he's gotta see you."

Fagin was angry and puzzled. "Now who . . ." He sighed. "Oh, hell, yes, I know who it is. That fucking Dobbs busted out of the hospital." He shook his head in a resigned manner. "Bring the AWOL sonofabitch up here."

Ten minutes later, Archie Dobbs stood in the office. He didn't waste a breath. "Looky here, goddamn you, Fagin! Get my ass back out in the field with the detachment."

"Shut up making demands, Dobbs," Fagin said. "How the hell did you get over here to Peterson Field anyhow?"

"I came with a work detail, but that's beside the point," Dobbs said.

Fagin pointed to the warrant officer. "Do you know—"

Dobbs sneered. "Fuck him. I want to get back to the mission."

Fagin grinned. "That's a hell of a way to talk about the guy that saved your life, Dobbs. He came in on a hot LZ to medevac your worthless ass out of there."

Dobbs was impressed. "Yeah? I was kinda conscious at the time. That was a hell of a thing."

The warrant officer walked over and extended his hand. "The name's Erick Stensland."

Dobbs shook his hand. "Well, hell. There's not much to say but thanks."

"I was just doing what they pay me for," Stensland replied.

Fagin interrupted with a wagging finger in Archie's direction. "Right now, asshole, I'm trying to get a flight cleared to get some contact with the guys. I don't know where they are. You can just pull up a chair and sit tight to sweat this out with Erick and me."

"Sure," Dobbs said, understanding the situation. He went over to the refrigerator and got himself a beer.

"You're welcome," Fagin said sarcastically.

Dobbs ignored the CIA man. He sat down and smiled at Stensland. "What outfit are you in?"

"I'm attached to SOG," the pilot answered. He noted Archie's accent. "You're from Boston, right?"

"Cambridge, actually," Archie said. "But certainly not a Harvard man."

"I call Knee Lake, Minnesota home," Stensland said.

"Product of the solid Midwest, are you?" Archie remarked. "Say! I'll fucking bet that was a hell of a job of flying you did when you lifted me out of the operational area."

"I saw your guys drawing fire out in the open," Stensland said. "They really inspired me."

The phone rang. Fagin quickly grabbed it and answered. He listened to a few words on the other end before he spoke. "That's fucking rotten," he said. He hung up. "That was our last chance."

"What's the matter?" Archie asked.

"The brass won't give clearance for any searches for Falconi," Fagin said.

Archie jumped to his feet. "Well, I'm gonna find a way to help out."

"Look at you!" Fagin exclaimed. You're not in good enough shape to do any field work. What the hell do you think you can do?"

"I don't know what," Archie shouted angrily, "but whatever it is, it'll be more than you'll try!" He chug-a-lugged the half-full can of beer. After an angry glare at the CIA case officer, he stormed out of the office.

Archie rushed down the hall to the stairs and took them two at a time down to the first floor. He'd reached the front door when a wave of nausea swept over him. He had to wait a couple of moments for his head to clear. The he heard his name called from behind.

It was Stensland.

"Whew!" the warrant officer said. "You move fast, don't you?"

"You'll have to pardon me, bud," Archie said impatiently. "I ain't got all the time in the world." He started to walk away but Stensland grabbed him. Archie angrily jerked away. "Leave me go, man!"

"I have a chopper," Stensland said. "And I'll fly that pretty mama any fucking place in the world."

Archie was suddenly interested. "Yeah? You ain't too worried about proper flight clearances, huh?"

"Hell, no," Stensland said. "And I got a permanent fuel chit for Nui Dep."

Archie uncharacteristically became the picture of miliary courtesy. "Mister Stensland, I'd appreciate anything you could do. Really, sir!"

Stensland smiled easily. "Call me, Erick."


The Algerians changed their concentrated attack tactics later that afternoon. They pulled back and began a series of minor probes that would suddenly break the enforced silence of the jungle with yells and volleys of fire, then go quiet until the next assault.

Falconi had a conference of war with Top Gordon, Chris Hawkins and Ray Swift Elk. He pointed to their exact position on the map, then moved his finger to another point where the contour lines suddenly bunched in close together. "That's a bluff," he said. "I we could get to that spot, with that baby to our backs we'd be able to cut down the amount of defensive perimeter we'd have to cover."

Top was in agreement. "Sure, Skipper. But how the hell are we going to get over there? You said yoursel that the only reason me and my Bravo team busted i here was because they let us."

"That's right," Falconi said. "They wanted us all bunched up together for an easier, quicker kill."

Ray Swift Elk grinned at his commander. "You got something in mind, don't you?"

"Yep," Falconi said. He shoved the map over to the Sioux Indian. "Get an azimuth on that exact location. We're going over there."

"Yes, sir!" Swift Elk replied. He didn't know how Falconi could pull it off either, but he had enough faith in his commander not to question him. "I'll have it worked out in two shakes."

Chris Hawkins frowned in puzzlement. "I don't understand, Skipper. If we couldn't break out of here before, how're we going to do it now?"

"I've got an idea," Falconi said. He nudged Top. "Tell Calvin and Blue to get their asses over here — and bring the Claymores." He turned back to Chris. "Of course, it might not work."

Swift Elk looked up from his chore. "Then we'll all die one way or the other today."

# Chapter 17

Several swarms of bullets, coming from several directions, cracked above the Black Eagles and passed over their heads. Falconi's men instinctively pressed themselves closer to the ground as some of the projectiles slapped into tree trunks or tore off bits of bark and twigs. Other rounds zinged off into empty air, buzzing angrily away.

This was the Algerians' way of letting the detachment know they were still under plenty of firepower.

Calvin Culpepper, ducking with each new salvo, scrambled as rapidly as possible through the brush. He kept up the perilous trek from the perimeter to the center of the formation until he reached the spot where Falconi waited for him.

Calvin, his ebony face shiny with beaded sweat, reported in without ceremony. "Them Claymores is set up, sir."

"How many?" Falconi asked.

"An even dozen, Skipper," Calvin answered. "Blue is ready to detonate ever' one o' the fuckers electrically when you give the word." He shook his head slowly. "Damn, sir. Them things is dangerous to the rear too. There's a backblast of sixteen meters."

"I know," Falconi said. "By the book, all personnel within a hundred-meter distance of the rear and sides are supposed to be under cover."

"Shit, sir!" Calvin exclaimed. "We ain't got but seventy or seventy-five meters across this whole damn perimeter of ours. We're really taking a chance."

"We don't have any choice. The guys are going to have to dig in and get behind trees and every other piece of cover they can find," Falconi said. "There's no other way to do it, Calvin. We're taking a big risk, granted, but it's either that or die in here like cornered rats."

Calvin glanced back to the west side of their positions. The Claymores—officially designated as M18A1 Directional Mines—were set to blast outward into one side of the Algerian formation. Falconi's game plan was simple: set off the twelve explosive devices that would throw a grand total of eighty-four hundred steel balls, plus concussion, blast and secondary missiles, at the attackers. Then the Black Eagles were to slug their way through the opening created by the detonation. After that they had to reach the location of bluffs some two hundred meters away. Once there, they could dig in and set up a stronger position by using the higher ground behind them as cover.

The black demo man shrugged. "We're kinda like that ol' preacher man that was run up a tree by a big ol' bear. He prayed and said, 'Lord, if you can't help me, please don't help that bear!' "

Falconi laughed. "I suppose I could pray and say, 'Lord, if you can't throw a lot out at the Algerians, please don't throw too much back at us.' Actually, all I can ask of our Maker is to let those Claymores function properly."

"They will, sir," Calvin promised him. "Me and Blue guarantee it. So I'll get on back to the boy and wait for the word to blow them beauties." He swiveled around on his belly and crawled away.

Top Gordon, his last stogie unlit and reduced to a stub, chewed on the cigar. He took it out of his mouth and spat. "What'll we do once we get to those bluffs, Skipper?"

"The same thing we're doing here," Falconi said. "Except we'll have the high ground to our rear. We can sure as hell put up a stronger defense if we don't have to cover so damned much territory."

Chris Hawkins carefully eyed his commander. He started to speak, but a sudden attack on the east side of their position broke out. He had to crawl off and check things out because his Alphas were manning that portion of the line. The fighting died down after a few minutes, and Chris returned to the CP area. When he got there, he found that Chief Brewster had packed up all the radio gear and was ready to move out.

Falconi lit a cigarette. "What was going on over there?"

"The same old shit," Chris said. "They're just playing with us by shooting up a storm or making quick probe into our lines." He shifted his M16. "Are we about ready, Skipper?"

"We'll make our break in another five minutes," Falconi said.

"I don't want to bring up any unnecessary conversation, sir," Chris remarked, "but you have something special on your mind, don't you?"

"Yeah," Falconi admitted. "I think if we can put up a stronger resistance it'll knock some of the cockiness out of those bastards. Those bluffs are the best place to do it. Once they're slowed down and more cautious, we can start infiltrating through their lines and reach that cached radio. Then we can call in a re-supply drop."

Top Gordon was puzzled. "The whole damned detachment is going to try it, sir?"

"A couple of guys at a time," Falconi said. "All of us

couldn't make it in one big rush."

"The first one or two teams might make it," Chris surmised, "but they'll need a hell of a lot of luck."

"The Black Eagles have always needed a hell of a lot of luck," Falconi said.

"The last bunch trying to leave is gonna get wasted," Top said. "The Algerians will have wised up to what's going on by then."

"That's you, Chris and me," Falconi said. "All we can do is hope we can make it, too."

Chris, ever the officer, kept his expression calm. "It's the only way."

"Jesus! RHIP—Rank Has Its Privileges—huh?" Top remarked with forced humor.

"You got it, Top," Falconi said. "Now you and Chris get back to your guys and get 'em ready to move. And, for God's sake, make sure they're plastered close to Mother Earth. The air around here is going to be full of all kinds of flying shit. I'm talking about stuff that'll take a man's head off!"

"Right, Skipper," Top said. He and Chris moved out of the CP area. Falconi gave them time to reach their teams, then picked up his Prick-Six and called in Ray Swift Elk. "Tell Calvin to blow those Claymores on my command—wait!"

"Roger," came back the Sioux Indian's voice.

Falconi timed one full minute with the sweep hand of his watch. After exactly sixty seconds, he spoke again. "Blow 'em!"

There was one solid second of silence, then the whole area blasted into a noisy, thunderous, dusty, windy, man-made storm. Pieces of dirt, vegetation and rocks shot through the air with the force of bullets. The area to the front of the Claymores was swept clean of all brush.

The exact moment the noise subsided, Ray Swift Elk

leaped up and charged forward. Top Gordon's Bravos crowded behind him with Falconi and Chief Brewster following. The back of the Black Eagle formation was made up of Chris Hawkins' Alphas. Kim and Bill Taylor were the rear guard who kept an eye on any baddies that might try to tag along.

Swift Elk grimaced at the first three mangled bodies he had to leap over. The trio of North Africans, who were blasted into hunks of red gore by whipping steel balls, were barely recognizable as having been human beings. The Sioux scout continued his advance, finding more butchered humanity.

He had to go almost fifty meters past mutilated corpses before he reached the first victims who had been far enough away from the blast to be only wounded by the shrapnel and other flying debris.

One of the Algerians, grimacing and growling, was a tough bastard. His left leg was gone but he had fashioned a tourniquet over the stump. When he saw Swift Elk, his rage overcame reason and he let his self-treatment of first aid go, grabbing for the AK47 lying nearby.

Swift Elk had no time to express his admiration of such guts. He simply swung the muzzle of his rifle in that direction and pushed three rounds into the guy. They all struck home—two in the chest, one in the face—and the Red flipped over into the pool of blood coming from the shattered leg.

Then more incoming rounds, sporadic but determined, splattered around the Black Eagle scout. He answered in kind and kept up the rush.

Falconi noted the resistance ahead. "Go for it, guys!" he yelled up to the Bravos. Behind him, Chief Brewster moved awkwardly but rapidly forward, his breath labored and rapid under the burden of the heavy radio he carried. Falconi glanced over at him, then back at the Alphas closing in tight behind them. The desperate looks in the men's eyes showed they fully realized the gamble they were taking at the moment.

All the chips were in the middle of the table, and the final bet made. There was one last card to play, and it would be dealt by old Mister Death—from his own deck.

Chief warrant officer Erick Stensland eased the Hughes OH-6A chopper down onto Camp Nui Dep's landing pad.

Archie Dobbs, seated behind the pilot in the open door of the gunner's position, leaned on the M60 machine gun mounted there and peered out over the isolated post. Somehow he hoped to see Falconi or Top Gordon standing there. But he was disappointed.

As soon as the skids were on the dirt, Archie slipped from the safety belt and leaped to the ground without waiting for Stensland to cut the motor. He trotted over to the bunker control tower. He squatted down and peered in at the Air Force sergeant inside. "Hey," Archie said, "any word on Falconi and his guys?"

"Not over my net," the man said. "Check with Major Riley's commo shack."

"You mean there ain't been any flights in or out of here that concerns the Black Eagles?" Archie asked.

"Not a one, pal," the Air Force sergeant replied. "And I'm the boy that runs this side of town."

"Christ! You'd think there'd at least have been a re-supply drop gone out for 'em."

"Nope," the guy insisted.

Archie stood up and rushed over to help Stensland tie down the chopper. They'd just finished when a jeep roared up to the landing pad. Major Riley leaped out and approached them. When he noted Archie, his mouth opened and he stopped in midstride. "Jesus, Dobbs! We heard you clobbered in."

Archie grinned. "Yeah, I rode a streamer into the DZ, but I guess I'm too damned dumb to know I'm supposed to be dead."

"Jesus, Dobbs!" Riley said, repeating himself. "Didn't you even get hurt?"

"I got shook up," Archie admitted. "They stuck me in the hospital at Long Binh, but I sort of walked away."

"AWOL, huh?" Riley remarked with a grin. He glanced over at Stensland and greeted him with a nod. "Are you tied up with these bastards now?"

"I suppose I am," Stensland answered.

Archie was in no mood for idle conversation. "Any word from Falconi yet?"

"Hell," Riley said. "I was about to ask you the same thing."

"It looks like things are as bad as I figgered," Archie said.

"That doesn't leave us any choice but to go looking for him," Sensland said.

"I agree," Riley said. "Since his commo capability seems to be all fucked up, that'll be the only way to contact him and his boys."

"The Air Force guy in the bunker told me they hadn't had any re-supply," Archie said. "Is that right?"

Riley shook his head. "Valverde's bundles are still rigged for delivery. There hasn't been any calls in since your medevac."

"Goddamnit!" Archie said. "They must be short of just about everything."

Stensland was anxious to get on with the job. "Let's pick up a couple of ammo bundles and hustle out there and see if we can find 'em."

Riley offered some advice. "I'm familiar with the operational area they're in. There's only a few places where drinkable water is available. You might consider substituting some jerry cans of good ol' H-two-O in place of at least one bundle of bullets."

"Good point, Major," Archie said. "We can handle two bundles in that bird. We'll take one of Hank Valverde's 5.56-millimeter loads for the M16s."

"And I'll have my S4 sergeant rig up a twenty-gallon delivery for you."

"OK," Archie said eagerly. "There's something I need from our bunker. There's an extra Prick-Six over there. It may be all we'll able to use to raise the detachment. Especially if their other commo gear is all fucked up. I'll run over and grab it."

Riley walked to the edge of the landing pad and shouted loudly over to his Green Beret supply bunker. "Hey! Bring over one of Falconi's M16 ammo bundles. Then rig up four jerry cans of water, and load the whole shit-and-caboodle on this chopper!"

A distant voice obediently responded in the affirmative.

"Go get that radio, Archie," Stensland said. "I'll see to getting the equipment stowed."

"Thanks, Erick," Archie said. Still a bit weak, he couldn't do much more than slowly trot across the camp toward the Black Eagle bunker.

Stensland turned his attention to the chopper, clearing away a place in the tiny rear area for the supplies.

The aircraft was officially designated as the Cayuse. Its 250-horsepower engine, an Allison T63 shaft-turbine, gave it a maximum speed of 160 miles per hour. The armament was simple but effective. An M60 machine gun was mounted for operation from the right door. That was Archie's battle station. An M134 Minigun, its six barrels capable of firing two thousand to four thousand of its 7.62-millimeter rounds per minute, was mounted on the left side where it was controlled by the pilot.

Archie's spot was directly behind the cockpit. The place was so small that he had to sit with his legs outside the door, and rest his feet on the skids. Here he acted as gunner, observer and aerial deliveryman. With a couple of Hank Valverde's equipment bundles in with him, there would barely be room for the Black Eagle.

Riley was better than his word. He provided a detail of men who quickly gathered up the supply load and brought it out to the helicopter. The Green Berets had the gear stowed when Archie returned from the bunker with the small radio.

The S4 sergeant and the other men had been among those brawling with the Black Eagles before they'd left on their present mission. It was obvious from their actions that there was no animosity in their hearts for Falconi or any of his men. The only thing on their minds was to help out some comrades in arms who were probably outnumbered and cut off deep in enemy territory.

Riley, smoking one of his cheap cigars, watched the final preparations. "I figured you'd be coming in low and making a free drop."

"Yes, sir," Archie said. "Or if we're lucky, we can just land and hand the stuff over in a more gentlemanly style."

"Don't count on it," Riley said. "There's some bad shit going down out there. We haven't been able to raise the relay station since the mission began. In fact, the only transmission we received was for your me-devac. From that point on, it's all been dead air."

Stensland pulled on his helmet. "I just hope we can find 'em, Major. According to the OPLAN they could be just about anywhere. They had no timetable or map points to worry about.

"That's us Black Eagles," Archie said. "We just go hunting until we find some ass to kick—no matter where it is."

"If they're out there, you'll make contact," Riley said.

"That's why I got the Prick-Six," Archie explained. "We'll be flying low enough to use this baby. Since they got theirs on, they'll either pick me up or I can monitor them eventually. Between Falconi's, the scout's and the fire teams, I got to hear something."

"And vice versa," Stensland said. He motioned to Archie. "The aircraft is ready for flight. Let's go."

"Right behind you," Archie replied. The two hurried over to the chopper.

"Hey!" Riley called after the departing pair.

"Yeah?" Archie yelled back.

"When you find Falconi, tell the sonofabitch he owes me a cold beer!"

Archie waved back, then crawled into the rear of the helicopter. Within a minute, the motor had kicked on and the rotors were spinning faster. Then Stensland lifted her off, and the small flying machine swerved through the air and headed out for the operational area.

# Chapter 18

Maj. Robert Falconi noted that Bravo Team's advance was slowing down. He almost caught up with Hank Valverde a couple of times, and had to slacken his own pace to avoid closing in on the grenadier. Not wanting to chance the detachment getting crowded together, he motioned back at the lead man of the trailing Alphas.

Calvin Culpepper saw the signal and understood the situation immediately. He also eased back and kept the same interval between himself and his commanding officer. He motioned to his teammates Bill Taylor, Chun Kim and Chris Hawkins, letting them know to slacken their speed. The three, having to tend to their own chores and also keep an eye on Calvin, had to keep every sense and nerve on alert. Although they were in the rear of the Black Eagle attack, there were plenty of chores on the flanks for them. The Algerians may have been surprised and shocked, but it wasn't long before they began to appear on the sides of the battle formation. Luckily for Falconi's guys, the North Africans were few enough to be either discouraged from coming closer or blown away altogether by the skillful application of M16 fire. This, of course, was augmented from time to time by a well-placed round from Kim.

Then the first real ammo crisis developed.

"Lieutenant Hawkins!" the Korean marine yelled over to the team leader. "Grenades pretty soon no more."

Chris blasted away at a fleeing figure in tan off to his left. When he was certain the man had either been hit or drawn off, he turned his attention to the grenadier.

"How many you got left, Kim?"

"I got three," Kim yelled. A flurry of shooting by Bill Taylor was heavier than usual. The Korean raised the M79 and arced a projectile that way. It detonated and the air was rent with the screams of wounded North Africans. Kim again called out to Chris. "Now I got two."

In the meantime, Falconi's frayed nerves were becoming a bit more unraveled at the slow progress of Top Gordon's men. He took his Prick-Six radio and angrily squeezed the transmit button. "Bravo! What the fuck's going on up there?"

"They're stacking up in front of us, Falcon," came back Top's voice. "And the vegetation is murder through here. It's slowing down the scout."

Falconi regretted his anger. He should have known that whatever was cutting down their attack's momentum would be something almost out of Top's or Swift Elk's control. But if action wasn't taken quickly, the Algerians would completely recover from the Claymore-induced breakout and crush them.

Falconi raised Top, Chris and Swift Elk on the Prick-Six. "Bravo, Scout. Hold up. Alpha, send your grenadier to me on the double. You continue forward. Out." As he spoke, the major increased his own pace until he once again could see Hank Valverde in the rear of Bravo Team.

"Roger, Falcon," Chris replied. "But he's only got two rounds left."

Falconi cursed under his breath, then called out to his supply sergeant. "Hank! How many grenades do you have?"

Valverde, surprised that Falconi was that close,

turned and waited for him to catch up. "I got four, sir."

"OK. When Kim comes up, give him one of yours. That way, you'll have three and he'll have three."

"Yes, sir," Hank said. "What gives?"

"We have to reach those frigging bluffs within fifteen minutes or lose the war," Falconi said. "You guys are going to be our artillery."

Kim, struggling through the thick brush, caught up with them. "Lieutenant Hawkins sent me to you, Falconi."

Falconi quickly explained what was wanted. While Kim got the projectile from Hank, the commander waited for the Alphas to catch up as quickly as possible.

It only took two minutes of struggling through the clinging vegetation before Chris, Calvin and Bill Taylor made an appearance. By that time the Bravos were halted, ready to have the entire detachment—the remaining seven men—join them. When the complete unit was formed up to his satisfaction, Falconi looked over at Kim and Hank.

"Gentlemen, do it to it."

The two grenadiers fired alternately, holding the M79s so the shells could be lobbed between the branches of nearby trees and land twenty meters ahead.

The explosions started with the same regularity as the delivery of the grenades. When the sixth detonated, the Black Eagles ran forward in a formation similar to the old Roman Legion *testudo*—turtle—which was a square of fighting men designed to withstand attacks from all sides while crashing through enemy lines. But instead of having shields and spears all around, there was a spray of deadly 5.56-millimeter fire.

The nearest Algerians, again caught unaware by the changing tactics of the Black Eagles, were swept away. Their more prudent buddies, smart enough to take

186

advantage of the good cover offered by the monsoon forest, fell back and returned the salvos from their Kalashnikov assault rifles.

The detachment swept through the area and bounded into the heavier brush of ground that slanted toward the base of the bluffs. Without orders, following soldierly instinct, they put the high ground to their backs and turned to face the attack that was sure to come

The Algerians didn't give them more than a couple of moments to wait.


Maj. Gen. Valdimir Kuznetz, Soviet KGB, stood at the front of the conference room and faced his audience. A large briefing map of Southeast Asia was mounted on the wall behind him. The meeting had just been called to order, and the Russian allowed a few moments for everyone to settle comfortably in their seats and light up. They had been quickly summoned from their quarters to attend the session. Their slightly disheveled appearances gave evidence of the haste with which they had arrived.

The main part of this group consisted of three other officers. All were the members of MOK—the Russian acronym for International Liberation Committee—a Communist tactical directorate under the direct command of Kuznetz. They were Col. Henryk Blinoski of Polish army intelligence, Col. Gyorgy Szako of the Hungarian State Police, and Col. Ngyun Lim, a commissar in the North Vietnamese army.

There were two other officers in the room, but they were not members of MOK. These were Lt. Col. Gregori Kraschchenko of the KGB, and his aide and translator Maj. Truong Van of the North Vietnamese army intelligence department. They sat in straight-backed chairs next to the far wall.

"Comrades," General Kuznetz announced, "the moment for which we have all been waiting has arrived."

Anticipating the good news, everyone in the room leaned forward. Krashchenko, on the other hand, sat rigid and anxious, his eyes puffy from lack of sleep. His mouth was hot and dry from chain-smoking, and a headache pounded in his temples like the sledgehammers in a Siberian salt mine.

Kuznetz continued. "I have received a radio message that is less than a half hour old. The Black Eagles — every one of the gangsters — are trapped in a culvert with a series of high bluffs to their rear." He turned and indicated the terrain features on the map. "As you can see here from the situation I have drawn on the acetate, they are surrounded on the other three sides by Major Ahmar's men. Also, with the relay radio station knocked out, they have absolutely no contact with their supporting echelons."

The Hungarian, Szako, clapped his hands. "Give the orders to crush them, Comrade General!"

"Wait!" cautioned Blinoski. "Remember we want to capture Falconi alive."

"Impossible!" snorted the NVA commissar, Ngyun. "He will commit suicide to avoid falling into our hands. There is every reason to believe that he has already taken cyanide capsules from his field medical kit and holds them ready for just such an act. Surely such orders were issued to him long ago."

"Comrade Ngyun is no doubt correct," Kuznetz said. "That is why I am about to issue an order to the Viet Cong battalion in the area to join in the battle to ensure victory."

"An entire battalion!" Blinoski exclaimed. "They will annihilate the Black Eagles — massacre them without mercy!"

"And that, comrades," Kuznetz said, "is exactly what we now want. There is too much to lose by holding back our firepower in hopes of taking any prisoners at all. The program for the internationalization of the people's struggle in Vietnam would fail. Therefore, Major Ahmar, reinforced by a battalion, will move in with but one order: Kill the Black Eagles."

Szako was satisfied. "There will be no problem doing that. After all, Falconi should be badly outnumbered by such a force."

"Approximately thirty-five to one," Kuznetz said.

"Wait!"

The officers turned toward the source of the shout. It was Krashchenko. Obviously agitated, he strode to the front of the room. "We must take Falconi prisoner," he insisted. "What about the show trial in Moscow? Don't forget, Comrade General, that he is a Soviet citizen by our law."

Kuznetz shook his head. "That consideration is now outweighed by others."

"We cannot kill him," Krashchenko pleaded. "The bastard must be humiliated for his crimes against socialism. Only by being shamed as a war criminal will true justice be served. Falconi's embarrassment will —"

Kuznetz smirked. "I find your choice of words interesting, Comrade Lieutenant Colonel Krashchenko. You say 'humiliated,' 'shamed' and 'embarrassed.' Was that not what Falconi did to you?"

Krashchenko trembled in rage. "I demand that Major Robert Falconi be dragged to justice like a pig to slaughter!"

"*Moltsani*—Silence!" Kuznetz roared. "The decision has been made."

"But, Comrade General!"

Kuznetz calmed down. "It is too late to argue, Krashchenko. Orders have already been issued, and

189

even now the first elements of the battalion have joined the Algerians. Falconi's destruction is only a matter of time."

Still shaking, Krashchenko backed away a few steps, then turned and strode out of the room. He turned down the hall, knocking orderlies and other soldiers aside as he hurried to his quarters. His mind swirled with disappointment, rage and fear. When he entered his room, Krashchenko slammed the door. He stood quietly for a few moments and finally fished his cigarette pack from his pocket. After lighting one, he walked over to the window and stared down at Hanoi's busy streets.

Lt. Col. Gregori Krashchenko felt that Falconi's death sentence was his own. As long as Falconi was in the operational area and exposed to capture, Krashchenko's life had a guarantee, albeit a shakey one, but the KGB brass had no reason to have him executed. If Falconi could be captured and brought in for trial, then Krashchenko would survive. Perhaps he would be posted to a position of exile as a guard commandant in some prison camp. But even being stuck out in the desolate Siberian wastes would be better than being shot.

However, if Falconi died — and there was no reason to think the Black Eagle commander could survive the crushing forces now prepared to destroy him and his unit — then Krashchenko would pay the full price for past failures and humiliations.

He'd learned to have a great deal of respect for the American major, but even Falconi could not break through such an overwhelming force.

Krashchenko went to his desk and pulled the To-karev pistol from the drawer. He also picked up a half dozen magazines, each loaded with eight 7.62-millimeter rounds, and slipped them into various pockets.

After checking the weapon to make sure there was a bullet chambered, he settled down on the chair to make a final decision on what he must do.


There was no more team integrity in the Black Eagles now. Their small line of defense was manned by individuals, their only weapons, now that the M79 grenade launchers were out of ammo, were their M16s.

The ammo supply for the rifles was down to the last rounds, too. Hank Valverde, in his role as supply sergeant, had made a quick inventory and reported back to Falconi.

"Sir, we're running with a couple of hundred rounds per man," Valverde reported through cracked, dried lips. "There's no more'n six hand grenades along us all, and no water."

Falconi took the news calmly. "Thanks, Hank. You can get on back to the perimeter now."

"Yes, sir." Hank had turned to crawl back, then had stopped and looked over his shoulder. "Hey, Major."

"Yeah?"

"Good luck, sir."

Valverde's words were meant to convey a sincere wish that whatever decisions were going to be made would be the best possible for everyone. It was a wish for good fortune for the whole detachment.

"Skipper," Chief Brewster said, crawling in from where he'd set up a quick commo station.

Falconi knew what the chief had to say from the expression on his face. "Couldn't raise shit, huh?"

The chief shook his head. "We couldn't reach Nui Dep with this PRC-77 if we had an antenna a thousand feet tall."

"OK. Thanks, Chief. We had to give it a try," Falconi

said.

"I ain't much good to you as a commo man, Skipper," the chief said. "Want me to go for'd and join the boys on the firing line?"

"Sure," Falconi said. "We could use an extra hand on the right side there."

"The starboard side? Aye, aye, sir."

Falconi watched the Navy man move off into the brush. He fished around in his pockets and found a smashed cigarette. The major twisted and smoothed it out, then stuck it in his mouth. The taste was bitter and added to his thirst.

His mind reflected the situation. Numb with fatigue and long hours of hellish fighting, Robert Falconi's conscious spoke to him from the depths of his soul:

*Well, old buddy, maybe this is it. You're short of ammo, long on thirst and out of luck. This is what your entire life has now boiled down to. Enlisting in the Army, the years in Korea, Officers' Candidate School, volunteering for Special Forces, forming the Black Eagles—all this, was just part of the funneling process that brought you down to a fucking gully in Cambodia. And now you have to make the one choice that every military commander in the history of mankind has prayed to his particular god or gods to keep him away from: Whether to surrender or die!*

The Prick-Six crackled, and Falconi recognized Swift Elk's voice. The Sioux had gone out as an advance picket in front of their positions. The Indian's voice was terse but calm. "Falcon. This is scout. VC are in the area now. Estimate battalion strength. I'm moving back into the perimeter. Out."

Falconi set the radio down, the terrible words now pounding in his head:

*Surrender or Die!*

# Chapter 19

The first wave of shrieking Viet Cong crashed through the jungle toward the Black Eagles like a horde of insane zealots. Packed inside the densely overgrown terrain, they came on almost shoulder to shoulder, presenting a solid wall of humanity to the weapons of Falconi's men.

Falconi had given the order to keep all weapons on semiautomatic in order to conserve ammo. Now the men's trigger fingers pumped in rhythmic spasms, sending single shots to slap into the mass of shouting Reds that crowded in on them.

The enemy took horrible casualties. The guerrillas of the Viet Cong battalion had been told that their opponents were like trapped cobras, unable to escape but deadly until killed. The sooner the gangsters were crushed, the sooner the battle would be over.

The dead began to pile up in front of the Black Eagles, and the pressure against them built in the swirling, smoking hell of the battle until the VC in the ensuing waves had trouble stumbling over the stacks of their dead and wounded comrades. This not only broke the momentum of their attack, but calmed them down a bit with the realization they were getting the living hell shot out of themselves. Their officers and squad leaders who had lost momentary control took advantage of the sobering experience to regain command of their troops.

Meanwhile, the Algerians made an appearance in the midst of the attacks. These North Africans had been in as much combat as the Black Eagles. They were more cautious than their VC comrades, and preferred to move forward in small, probing groups. Their method of fighting would cause the battle to cease completely for a few moments. Then it would flair up in some part of the line in a wild, deadly confrontation of blasting AK47 and M16 exchanges. That would quickly die out within three to five minutes when then Algerians pulled back to try somewhere else.

After an hour of this, the Algerians were relieved by the VC. The Viet Cong commander had harangued his troops into trying harder, but they had thought he meant to become even more aggressive. When the Red guerrillas again entered the fight, their leaders lost control of them once more. The men ran wild, mounting their screaming human-wave assaults, fully expecting to sweep over the Black Eagles or smash them against the bluffs to the rear.

Rifle barrels heated up to alarming temperatures as the regularly spaced independent fire raked the Communist assault lines, spilling the attackers to the ground in heaps of dead and near dead.

Sgt. Jake Bernstein, a holder of the Marine Corps expert rifleman's badge, maintained a controlled, well-spaced and accurate rate of fire. Hours of working out with weights in the gym had produced massively strong arms and shoulders that could keep the M16 up to his shoulder without tiring. And every round he shot found a living target across the space of jungle that separated him from the determined men trying to roll over or push him back farther to the bluffs.

The stack in front of Bernstein's position was particularly close packed and numerous. Most suffered from upper chest wounds — the exact spot where the Marine had aimed — and only a couple were wounded. The only break in his rate of fire was when a new magazine had to be inserted into the M16.

And that was when he died.

An Algerian sergeant, veteran of the war against the French, had stayed behind when his comrades withdrew to make room for the Viet Cong pressing in behind them. When the close-packed Red guerrillas attacked, Bernstein's full attention was drawn to them. The Algerian, well-concealed within a stand of bamboo, aimed carefully and fired.

The round hit Bernstein's temple, taking out the opposite side of his head. He made a quarter turn in the direction of the bullet's flight, then fell forward face-down onto the stinking jungle dirt.

His teammate Blue Richards had caught the movement in the bamboo, and seen Jake die. He ripped his remaining hand grenade from the pack suspenders, pulled the pin and flung it in a high arc. It sailed, hissing through the air, and crashed through the crackling vegetation.

The Algerian sergeant saw it coming and frantically leaped to his feet to run away from the deadly object. He misjudged the distance of the throw, however, and ran straight into the grenade. The shrapnel pulverized him from feet to chest. He collapsed, still living, into an undignified heap. He straightened out and attempted to crawl away, but his mangled body could not perform the movements demanded of it. The Algerian's life ended after long minutes of rolling around in agony, regretting the impetuous action that brought him to such a horrible situation.

Meanwhile, Falconi directed the battle from his little

command post which was no more than a depression in the earth with a large tree in front of it. The PRC-77 radio, no longer used by Chief Brewster, sat beside him. Turned on, the commo equipment hissed out the nothingness within its range. Men like Falconi never give up, however, and from time to time, he would squeeze the transmit button for a try at raising the radio back at Camp Nui Dep.

"Slick. Slick. This is Falcon. Over. Slick. Slick. This is Falcon. Over."

The results were the same. Nothing. If they'd been able to tote the big radio from the relay station, they could call in all the help they needed. But carrying the thing around was impossible, and would have interfered with their mission.

There was another problem too. The Black Eagles were now badly hurting from thirst. Tongues were beginning to swell, and the dryness in their mouths and throats made swallowing a painful chore. When any of the guys had to take a piss, all they could produce was a couple of weak, yellow drops. Dehydration, in this tropical hell, would progress more rapidly as the hours dragged on. Physical collapse and hallucinations were only a matter of time.

Food had only recently grown short. The C-rations were almost gone. It had been the fruit in the meals that had staved off thirst for so long. Although thick, syrupy and sweet, it had at least put some liquid in their bodies. But that was gone now. The rest of the chow, which consisted of cans of ham and eggs, pork sausage patties and beefsteak, would hardly be of benefit to bodies gone drier and drier over a period of days.

The ammo supply, too, was another factor. When that was gone, there would be nothing left but bayonets. And that was the question that Falconi faced:

Should the Black Eagles do the same as the Foreign Legionnaires in the Battle of Camerone? Faced with an overwhelmingly enemy, down to only a few men, out of ammo, mad with thirst, the legionnaires had mounted a bayonet charge into thousands of Mexicans.

Or should he surrender his command?

That, he knew after calm deliberation, was out of the question. The Communists had too many scores to settle with the Black Eagles. There would be no POW camp for the guys. Only trials as war criminals which would be followed by mass executions.

Even Clayton Andrews, when the Black Eagles were first formed for SOG, had told Falconi he'd be dragged off to Moscow if ever caught by the Reds. It had been quite a surprise for the detachment commander to find out that, since his mother had left Russia illegally without proper permits or exit visas, he was a citizen of the Soviet Union under their law.

The whole situation could be summed up by saying that, no matter what, it was a sure death for the Black Eagles.

Falconi made up his mind.

When the ammo was gone, it would be, Fix bayonets, charge! The lucky ones would die straight off, the less lucky would succumb to wounds, and the really unlucky survivors—if there were any—would be forced to go through the humiliation of a show trial before execution.

Falconi's thoughts were interrupted by a screaming, roaring explosion of noise. The Viet Cong were attacking again.

This time, the Reds' massed their firepower more effectively. Roaring swarms of 7.62-millimeter rounds whipped through the Black Eagle positions like packed clouds of steel hornets. The air cracked and split with the concussion.

Bill Taylor caught a round in the upper arm that blew his tricep muscle away. The force of the impact whipped him around to catch several more slugs in the upper back. The plucky Australian, his anger clouding over shock, rolled over and sat up. He grabbed his digger hat and sat it back on his head. Bill Taylor fired his M16 no more than six times before the next incoming shots blew him over on his back. He made no sound except to sigh aloud, then he died.

Falconi, from his position, was able to fire to all parts of the line. When he noted a growing pressure on one side, he added his own volleys of rounds to aid the guys there. The tree in front of his command post was bullet-pocked with all the bark blown away by the dense salvos slapping around him. When he finally noted that the enemy were building up all across the front, he grabbed the Prick-Six.

"Top, Chris, Ray! Move the guys back toward the CP."

There was no reply over their radios. Time didn't permit proper communications procedure. The three ranking men simply shouted orders and began the short withdrawal.

Chun Kim, stubborn and brave, moved slower than the rest. He emptied one magazine and crammed the last one he had into the M16. He had just pulled the charging handle to seat the first round when the grenade sailed over from the enemy positions.

It hit the ground and bounced. Kim grabbed it and flung it back toward the Reds, but it detonated a scant yard from his hand. The shrapnel blew back into his face and chest, the explosion rolling him over several times. Bloody and blinded, he lay in the dirt, no longer comprehending were he was.

Another grenade came in. This one finished the job, killing the brave Korean and taking away a man who was a veteran of six previous Black Eagles' missions.

At that same time the survivors formed up with a tighter perimeter, using their final bullets to throw back the pressing Communist attack. This extra spurt of firepower made the Reds break contact for a quick reorganization. Falconi took advantage of the lull to pass the word to Top and Chris.

"We're down to the nitty gritty here," he said grimly.

"Everybody's on their last magazines, Skipper," Top said.

"Yeah," Chris agreed. "We'll be throwing rocks next."

"We'll form up for a bayonet charge," Falconi said, not wanting to waste precious seconds. "When we advance we'll cut loose with our final rounds, then close with the sons of bitches. This is it."

It was a time for some classic final words, but no one could think of any. Whatever emotions or thoughts ran through the men's minds, they were the same experienced by the last guys standing at the Alamo, by Custer's command, or hundreds of other little battles where all was lost save the defenders' courage.

Falconi wiped at his filthy, sweat-streaked face and looked at his command. He loved those sons of bitches. These guys were the types that made up Caesar's Legions, Viking raiders, Napoleon's Imperial Guard, Britain's Thin Red Line, and all the other units that always gave a hell of a lot more of their sweat and blood than was asked of them. They would still fight bitterly in a situation where normal men would throw up their hands and surrender, or turn tail and flee to the rear.

Falconi licked his dried, cracked lips. His voice, though a bit hoarse with thirst, was still loud and clear. He wanted the goddamned Reds on the other side of that stinking stand of bamboo to hear this, his final command:

*"Fix bayonets!"*

199

There was shuffle of gear, then nine distinct clicks as that many bayonets were locked onto the studs of the M16 rifles.

Then the radio crackled to life.

"Falcon. Falcon. This is Archie. Over."

Every Black Eagle's eyes snapped over to the PRC-77. Expressions of disbelief were formed under the grime of jungle and battle that mottled their faces.

Falconi's hand shot out, grabbing the handset. "Archie. This is Falcon. Over."

Archie's voice, a bit distorted, was loud and clear. "Hi ya, Skipper. I'm in a chopper looking for you guys. Got ammo and water. Need any now? Over."

Hank Valverde was ever the good supply man. When an opportunity for re-supply presented itself, even in the midst of a losing battle, he was damned good and ready. The Chicano pulled a signal grenade off his harness. "Tell him to watch for red smoke!" He tossed the device over by the bluffs. Immediately a thick cloud of bright red smoke boiled up and rolled skyward.

"Find the red smoke and drop what you have on us," Falconi said. "And this area is definitely not under our control."

"Roger, Skipper," Archie replied. "We got a gunship here so we can lend some fire support. How does an extry M60 and a minigun sound to you?" He paused a minute. "Hey! I see the smoke. Are you guys in front of them cliffs there?"

"Roger," Falconi replied.

"Jesus!" Archie said. "How'd you dumb bastards get yourselves cornered like that?"

"How about odds of thirty-plus to one? But never mind, wiseass," Falconi replied. "I just hope that's a free drop you got rigged up for us. Parachutes might drift over to the enemy."

200

"Roger. We're coming in. Keep your heads up. I don't want nobody to get hit on the noggin."

There was no need to give any orders to the experienced veterans. With their final magazines locked and loaded, they moved out to meet whatever attack would be coming their way.

The Black Eagles didn't have long to wait.

The sound of the helicopter had been heard by the Reds. They knew it was now or never to make this final crushing attack on Maj. Robert Falconi and his men. Ahmar, the Algerian commander, turned to the Goryonov machine gun that had been supporting the attacks. He yelled at the two-man crew. "Prepare for anti-aircraft operation!"

The men quickly worked to rearrange the wheel mounts to change the weapon into an anti-aircraft mode.

When the chopper came in, it flew low, heading at a line of flight perpendicular to the Communist positions. From the automatic weapons' position, it was a perfect target. The gunner set up the lead he wanted, then began a slow, methodical tracking as he pressed the trigger.

The streams of heavy slugs, the tracers giving ample evidence of their accuracy, flew out at the aircraft in a perfect trajectory.

# Chapter 20

Sparks popped across the helicopter's fuselage, and a faint rattling of striking bullets could barely be discerned over the noise of the engine. Archie, his eyes riveted on the ground while he judged the proper distance prior to kicking the door bundles free, could sense the incoming rounds that danced through the same air where the helicopter flew.

Erick Stensland expertly worked the combination of cyclic, collective and rudders as he controlled the aircraft's rapid descent to both the proper altitude and location for the drop. The tops of trees were now buffetted by the chopper's downdraft, sending swirls of dust and leaves spinning through the violent machine-made winds.

Archie Dobbs, taking no notice of the terrain other than the spot where the Black Eagles detachment was supposed to be located, waited until they were several hundred feet in front of the thickest clouds of red smoke. At the right moment, he pushed the cargo hard with his foot. The little OH-6A chopper surged upward a bit at this sudden relief of weight. Then Archie glanced out toward the enemy's positions. He spoke angrily into the microphone on the flight helmet.

"Did you see where them rounds dancing around u

are coming from?"

Chief warrant officer Erick Stensland pointed back of them. "Yeah. The fucker's using tracers. I'll swing around again to draw his fire. Once he cuts loose, we'll go in with the mini gun."

"And the M60," Archie added, patting the machine gun that sat between his legs.

The two bundles crashed through the tree limbs, spinning crazily before slamming into the soft earth.

"Goddamn!" Malpractice McCorckel yelled. "That fucking Archie wasn't kidding when he told us to duck our heads."

Hank Valverde's supply detail—made up of him, Calvin Culpepper and Blue Richards—raced through the brush to where the bundles lay at the base of the bluffs. They quickly piled one on top of the other and lugged them back to the command post.

The trio reached the spot where Falconi, Top and Chris waited. Suddenly, bullets crashed into the trees around them.

*"Hijos de sus chingadas madres!"* Hank cursed in Spanish. "Them fuckers don't cut us no slack at all." He didn't bother to do any unbuckling or unstrapping. His GI Survival knife slit through the bundles, opening them. Bandoleers were quickly pulled out and tossed out to the Black Eagles on the shortened perimeter a few meters away.

Calvin Culpepper opened the first jerry can and lugged it from man to man. He began filling canteens rapidly, wasting a lot of water. But the situation was a pressing one that offered damned little time for neatness or efficiency. The fight was building up again. The fighters, suffering from horrible thirst, had to get some liquid in them pronto.

Within five minutes the full fury of the Viet Cong attack hit them. But fresh magazines pushed their contents of 5.56-millimeter rounds up into chambers as the Black Eagles hosed hundreds of rounds of the freshly acquired ammo into the attackers.

And they did it on full fucking automatic!


Stensland tilted the chopper into a nose-down position and cranked the throttle, pushing forward on the cyclic. The machine dove toward the portion of the jungle from where tracers of machine gunfire streaked up. The pilot held off to the last minute, then he hit the firing button on the M134 minigun. Its two thousand round per minute firing slashed at the exact position of the anti-aircraft opposition.

When he passed over the spot, Stensland banked steeply to allow Archie a chance to use the M60. The Black Eagle could see troops under the canopy of trees, so he raked them with long fire bursts until the helicopter had flown out of range.

"Let's go again!" Archie shouted over the intercom.

"Hang on, baby!" Stensland shouted back. He kicked the rudder and swung around to make another attack.


The Black Eagles had instinctively returned to their original fire teams with the fresh issue of ammunition. They had knocked down the initial VC onslaught, forcing the Reds to pull back and regroup with a hell of a lot less men than they had begun with.

Canteens full of the lukewarm water that Archie had dropped in on them, were turned up and the contents gurgled down dry throats.

"Take it easy!" Malpractice McCorckel had warned

them when he noted the hard and fast drinking. The medic fully understood the consequences of such rash action. "You dumb fuckers are gonna make yourselves sick."

But both Blue Richards and Calvin Culpepper were vomiting by then. Their bodies, while nowhere near death, had dehydrated enough that it was impossible for the tissues to absorb the amount of water poured into them.

The two, red-faced with both embarrassment and the results of gagging, wiped their mouths in time to hoist their M16s for the next shouting assault from the VC.

The dead in front of the Black Eagles were already stinking to high heaven. Bodies, grotesquely swollen by gases produced from decaying internal organs, turned black in the tropical heat. When stray rounds hit the cadavers, putrid flesh exploded outward like solid pus from lanced boils.

But the Viet Cong struggled across the mass of rotting bodies in their frenzy to reach the Black Eagles. Interweaving streams of bullets hosed them down until the survivors drew off once again to regroup.

Then the Algerians, more cautious, advanced slowly in the cover provided by the forest. Leapfrogging forward, their fire was skillfully directed by officers and sergeants who sought to inflict casualties while conserving their own numerical strength. While this put less pressure on Falconi's men, it also provided fewer and more difficult targets in the monsoon forest brush.

The battle, showing every indication of getting bloodier, seemed to be building toward a decisive climax which, at that particular time, offered neither side a real solid chance for victory. There was only one thing for sure:

The losers would never walk away from the site. And

most of the winners would also be left to join the rotting dead.


Maj. Omar Ahmar was more worried about the helicopter than the enemy on the ground. He had a pathological hatred of the machines and the men who flew in them. The war in Algeria would have been much easier for the FLN if it hadn't been for those *mal'un* Allouette helicopters used by the French.

Back in those days, he and his fellow rebels would raid a village, kill the local civil leaders and the few Arab collaborators, then pull back to the mountains to escape the colonial paras and the legion. They would spend days traveling steep, rocky terrain that exhausted them to tears as they headed for their hideouts. Once they neared their sanctuaries, the damned choppers would come swooping in to drop off the determined paratroopers who were fresh and eager after a short flight. Ahmar and his men, under this unrelenting pressure, generally got the worst of it, with the survivors barely escaping from the pincerlike maneuvers of the attackers.

Ahmar saw the chopper make a turn, preparing to come in for another attack. The Algerian looked over at the crew of the Goryonov machine gun that had been altered to act as an anti-aircraft weapon. He pointed at the incoming helicopter and screamed, "*Rauwah banduk!* Destroy the bastard!"

The gunner pulled back on the crank while his loader steadied the belt of ammo ready to be pulled into the receiver. As soon as the chopper made its final turn, they tensed and waited.

Ahmar watched in anticipation as the helicopter came in lower, then leaped forward with a burst of speed. He gave his gun crew another glance, and shouted encouragement to them. "It will be easier than falling off a camel's back, comrades. Knock the flying pig out of the sky!"

The gunner raised the barrel and prepared to fire as the helicopter drew closer. The loader, also anxious, tensed and instinctively raised the belt of ammo.

Ahmar cheered aloud again. He turned to look at the two men. Suddenly the sky exploded and a windstorm of flying tracers and lead slammed into the machine gun's position. The crew flew apart in this hellacious metal tempest, the body parts splattered into the forest behind them.

Erick Stensland's minigun had spoken again.

Ahmar's mouth was open wide in horrified astonishment. A functioning, well-trained pair of gunners had been manning a skillfully manufactured automatic weapon. Then, in only a few seconds of a blasting inferno, they had been turned into mutilated nothingness. Ahmar could only stare at the red smears and hunks of human meat smashed against the tree trunks.

Master Sgt. Top Gordon was positioned behind his Bravo Fire Team. The Bravos were numerically better off than the Alphas. Top had three men under his command, and he had arranged them so that their combined fire crisscrossed and intermixed along the point of the line where the attackers were the most numerous. The master sergeant, now being the only man keeping his M16 on full automatic, added firepower where needed with short bursts that added punch to his team's efforts.

The Viet Cong, still massing in the hopes of overwhelming the Black Eagles by the sheer weight of numbers, hit this side of the perimeter the hardest. They climbed over the stacks of their dead and dying comrades to leap down onto the short space of open terrain in front of the Bravo positions. From here they surged forward into the combined firing that swept them away in groups of four and five at a time. A carpet of their dead now spread out from the larger pile of cadavers forward toward Top and his guys.

Yet, despite these losses, the Viet Cong had begun to gain ground. Top raised Falconi on his Prick-Six. "Falcon. This is Bravo. The Charlies have found a widening in the trees in front of us. They're starting to build up the pressure here. We need some support fire from the chopper. Over."

"Roger, Bravo," Falconi said coming back. "You got any smoke? Over."

"A green smoke grenade," Top replied. "Over."

Falconi's reply was businesslike. "Throw the motherfucker to your immediate front. Out." He kept the Prick-Six handy for any more calls from his team leaders, but turned his attention to the PRC-77. "Chopper," he said. "This is Falcon. Give us a couple of good runs in front of the green smoke. Over."

Chief warrant officer Erick Stensland wheeled the chopper around. "I don't see any—oh! There it is! Roger, Falcon."

Archie, who had monitored the exchange over his helmet headset, gave a cheer that was whipped away in the rotor blast. "Kick ass, goddamnit! *Calcitra clunis!*"

Stensland, however, picked it up over his own earphones. "What the hell? Are you speaking Latin?"

"Sure," Archie replied. "You didn't know you had a scholar riding shotgun, did you?"

"A regular college graduate, huh?"

Archie laughed into the intercom. "Yeah! The College of Hard Knocks. I got a Ph.D."

"Fuck academia," Stensland said. "Just remember when I pull out of the attack we'll be exposed to ground fire. Make your work on that M60 earn good grades."

The chopper tipped forward, then went in for the attack.



The remnants of the Viet Cong battalion formed up under the shrieking orders of its enraged commander. He had suffered sixty percent casualties in a battle that was supposed to have been won in a single, crushing mass attack.

There were now almost three hundred of his men lying in the bloody mountain of pulverized bodies in front of the gangsters' positions. He had given stinging blows across the face to every surviving officer and noncommissioned officer he could lay his hands on. He screamed in their faces of what failures they were to the cause of international communism. Orders from Hanoi had stated how important it was to destroy the capitalist running dogs dug in at the foot of those bluffs.

Vietnamese honor was at stake here too.

The Algerians, visitors to this war that belonged to the VC, had been doing better. The North Africans were getting chewed up too, but not a quarter as bad.

The Red cadre, their faces stung from the slaps they had received, in turn punched and kicked their own men for this final effort. When all was ready, the battalion commander stepped forward to give the order to attack. He noted the green smoke through the forest.

"You see?" he bellowed in his falsetto voice. "The stupid *lira* have marked their positions to make it easy for us to hit them head-on. *Dirng so*—don't be afraid! This will be the final charge of the battle for us!"

The company commanders gave the orders and the battalion, packed close together, moved through the trees, their weapons ready to deliver the massed fire so effective within forest confines.

Then suddenly the very air they breathed blew apart in a roaring, thundering hail. It hit their ranks with such intensity that the men who came under this fire seemed to melt.

This inferno ended with the diminishing roar of a helicopter motor, and the VC pushed forward again. This time the incoming rounds came from the front, sweeping back and forth across the advanced squads.

The main body of the unit was on top of the largest pile of dead when once again the sky seemed to open up and slam flaming death and destruction into their midst.

The battalion commander's life was blown away like the suds on a trooper's beer. His mangled body joined the others of his destroyed command that littered the shattered forest glen.

The minigun does not giveth, it taketh away— completely!

# Chapter 21

Ali Mamoud, a loyal Communist volunteer for the Vietnamese project, committed suicide.

The Algerian sergeant had been acting strange for the previous few days, speaking bitterly of disappointments and broken promises. In fact, he had been so disloyal in some of his remarks that several younger members of the unit complained about it. But Maj. Omar Ahmar figured the combination of heat and combat fatigue had badly affected Mamoud's morale, and credited that to his flagging enthusiasm.

It was the major who found the body a hundred meters behind the main battle lines.

The Algerian force was well beaten by then. Those that weren't casualties had melted away into the jungle under the leadership of the junior officers. Ahmar had bid them goodbye and good luck. He was wrung out himself, and discouraged to the point that he didn't really give a damn what happened after that.

Ahmar stumbled away from the battle zone, not really caring where he was going, when he found Mamoud. The sight of the body was the last straw. Now, exhausted and morally crushed, he slumped down and sat by the dead man.

Sergeant Mamoud and Ahmar were old comrades. Both had served in the French army in Indochina, though Mamoud had been in a crack Algerian *Tirailleur* battalion and the two hadn't been acquainted at that time. But they had gone through the hell in the Aures Mountains together as Red members of the FLN, fighting hundreds of desperate little battles which slowly but surely chewed away the numerical strength of their rebel company. When DeGaulle gave Algeria to the insurgents, both men had been bleary eyed with combat fatigue — exactly as had happened to them now in Vietnam — their fighting attitude and physical strength sapped from long years of pressure put on them by the relentless forces of the fierce paras.

Ahmar glanced at Mamoud's corpse as he squatted there. The sergeant had done himself in by removing his boot and sticking a big toe through the trigger guard of the Kalashnikov. Being on semiautomatic, the weapon had fired once, sending the bullet through his lower jaw to exit out the top of his head. Blood, gore and brains were splashed more than five meters outward from the shattered skull.

The suicide victim's pack had come open and a small book had spilled out onto the ground. Ahmar absent-mindedly picked it up and glanced at it. His eyes opened wide in surprise when he noted it was a copy of the *Koran*.

What would a dedicated international communist like Mamoud be doing with the holy book of Islam? Had he begun to backslide that much in his devotion to Marxism? The book flipped open to the pages that Mamoud had been reading the most. Ahmar's gaze went to what was written there:

*In the Name of Allah, the Compassionate, the Merciful, the All-Knowing, who forgives sin and accepts repentance.*

Ahmar read on, now understanding that Mamoud had indeed gone back to the religion taught him in his childhood. It was as if he had sensed defeat all along.

Whatever terrors dwelt in Mamoud's heart, the sergeant had sought solace in the *Koran*.

Ahmar could recall his old village's own Moslem clergyman, and the lessons he taught to the people. All came from that same holy book, in which every phase and aspect of a True Believer's life was covered in detail.

Ahmar, now defeated with his men either dead or fleeing through the jungle, settled into a more comfortable position by the cadaver of his old comrade and continued to peruse the scriptures passed down from the prophet Mohammed. At first he found it difficult to concentrate. The circumstances of again being roundly trounced in battle, and in intermittent fever that had been bothering him for the past week, made his mind whirl from time to time. But, at last, his mental condition calmed, and he could fully comprehend the lessons.

He continued studying, his burning brain absorbing it all, until a Truth came to him. Although it was deep within his psyche, it hit him with the same intensity of an exploding eighty-one-millimeter mortar shell. Once again, as during his early youth, Omar Ahmar believed in Allah the Compassionate, the Merciful. His spent mental processes produced theories that this mission back to Indochina had been brought about by Allah to enlighten him.

Ahmar even felt the message stirring in him. He was forgiven, but he had a final mission on this earth to perform before he would be lifted from the misery of mortal beings to a paradise where the tenets of Islam promised that seven beautiful women waited to serve and pleasure him.

Ahmar's final duty on this earth would be to conduct a one-man *Jihad*—Holy War!

Maj. Robert Falconi and his men were infidels. In

the *Koran* it spoke of such men as the Heirs of Hell, and they must be destroyed. Ahmar felt the burning of religion boiling up from his soul; he stood up holding the AK47 high above his head in one hand with the *Koran* in the other.

His fever-racked mind told him that Allah wanted him to make a final mortal gesture to cleanse his soul once and forever, and do it in the name of all True Believers. It was as clear as the sound of the enemy helicopter that still circled overhead.

"There is no god but Allah!" he yelled as his voice grew louder and higher in pitch. "And Mohammed is His prophet!" He cranked a round into the Kalashnikov's receiver, then went forward toward the Black Eagle positions.


Krashchenko's hand shook as he poured a large splash of vodka into the glass. He slurped it down, feeling the strong drink burn its way down his gullet to his empty stomach. He took several deep breaths, then treated himself to three more quick shots. The alcohol warmed him, easing the mental tension that kept his brain tied up in knots.

But he jumped straight out of his chair at the knock on the door.

The Russian cleared his throat and forced himself to calm down. *"Da?"* he said in Russian, then quickly added one of the few phrases he knew in Vietnamese. *"Moi ong vao."*

The caller did as he was invited, and entered the room. It was a young Vietnamese orderly. He stood at attention and saluted. *"Monsieur le Colonel,"* he informed him, *"Monsieur le General* wishes to speak to you."

Krashchenko rubbed a hand across his unshaved chin. "The general, eh? *Da, da*, I will go to him presently."

The soldier went to the door, but looked back when he reached it. *"C'est très important, did Monsieur le General,"* he added before leaving the room.

Krashchenko smiled without humor. "I'll wager it's important," he said. The KGB officer went to his desk and pulled the Tokarev pistol out of the drawer and stuck it in his trouser waist. After shoving some extra magazines in the pockets, he left the room.

The Vietnamese officers and soldiers in the hallway were a bit alarmed at the sight of the big Russian lumbering down the hall muttering to himself in angry whispers. They sensed the combination of fear and hatred in the man.

"Kuznetz is *tsatki* if he thinks I'll just walk calmly to some wall and let a firing squad blast me," Krashchenko mumbled angrily. When he reached the general's office, he allowed the military secretary to announce him, then he lurched inside the room and stood in front of his commanding officer.

General Kuznetz frowned at the man looking across his desk. Bleary eyed, stooped and sporting a three-day growth of beard on his jaw, the officer looked like he'd just come off a three-day bender.

"Krashchenko! You're a mess."

"Yes, Comrade General," Krashchenko said, easing his hand toward the pistol.

"And you're drunk, too!"

"Only a little, Comrade General," Krashchenko said. "I am able to conduct myself properly."

"Well, never mind," Kuznetz said. He got up and walked to the window, his back toward the other Russian. "I have news from the field." He turned. "The Algerians were badly defeated. A few survivors reached a Viet Cong outfit north of their area of operation. Once again Falconi has triumphed."

Krashchenko sniffed angrily, wiping at his nose. "I told you we should have eased back and tried to capture him."

Kuznetz nodded. "Yes. You were absolutely correct, of course."

"Huh?" Krashchenko was surprised.

"There have been too many mistakes made in handling this entire Black Eagle problem," Kuznetz continued, "and KGB Operational Headquarters has decided that we've depended far too much on our North Vietnamese comrades."

Krashchenko smirked. "I said that before, too."

"Yes. It is a matter of record," the general said. "So we are going to take your advice. A detachment of elite volunteers consisting of Russians will be especially formed and trained with the one mission of capturing Robert Falconi and destroying his command."

"That is what was needed all along," Krashchenko said. His hand rested on the pistol beneath his loose shirt. He was damned good and ready to start shooting the moment any squad of guards broke into the room to arrest him. Krashchenko planned on making Kuznetz his first victim.

"And you are going to command the unit," Kuznetz said. "Transportation back to the Soviet Union has already been arranged."

Krashchenko's hand slipped from the Tokarev. "I don't understand."

"It's quite simple, Krashchenko," Kuznetz snapped. "An elite unit, exactly like Falconi's own detachment, is going to be created of handpicked Russian servicemen. They will be volunteers from the army paratroops, the navy infantry, the KGB and even the Border Guard. You, as their commander, will test and train them. Then return to Vietnam and go against Falconi and his Black Eagles."

Krashchenko smiled widely. A feeling of grateful relief flowed through his Slavic soul. He had withdrawn completely from the weapon. "Thank you, Comrade General."

"You are perfectly motivated for the job," Kuznetz said. "It was a waste to have you sitting around here rather than going into the field after those imperialists."

"Yes, Comrade General."

"It will take you between six months and a year to be ready," the general said. "I suggest you begin as quickly as possible."

"I shall pack now," Krashchenko said. He saluted, then went toward the door.

"Krashchenko!" Kuznetz exclaimed.

The colonel turned. "Yes, Comrade General?"

"Sober up."

Krashchenko grinned viciously. "I already have."

# Chapter 22

Chuck Fagin and Major Riley stood at the edge of the helicopter landing pad. They sipped beer from cans while watching the slow approach of two choppers coming into Camp Nui Dep.

"Who's the pilot on that Loach?" Riley asked.

"Stensland," Fagin answered. "I figured you might know him."

"Not really. I've seen him before and I only jawed with him a little while when he and Archie dropped in to pick up a supply drop for Falconi," Riley said. "You seem to be well acquainted with him though."

"Yeah," Fagin said. "He's done a hell of a lot of flying for SOG. I swear the guy could thread a needle with a chopper. That's why I picked him for the Medevac mission that brought Dobbs out of the field."

"The grapevine says he went in on a hot LZ without as much as batting an eye," Riley remarked.

"Yep. Stensland's got balls alright, and he's going to be doing one hell of a lot of flying for the Black Eagles from now on."

Riley, who knew the detachment's casualty rate, shook his head. "That's a death sentence, Fagin."

"Why should he be any different than the others?"

The two aircraft were overhead now. Stensland's smaller craft orbited while the larger H34 came in for a dust-swirling, roaring landing. Fagin and Riley walked under the whirling rotors after the wheels touched down. The Special Forces major noted the four bodies, wrapped in ponchos, lying on the chopper deck.

Falconi stepped out onto the dirt as the engines were cut. After Stensland landed a few meters away, he also powered down. The sudden cessation of noise created a strange silence over the scene.

Riley pointed to the dead men. "Lost four, huh?"

"Three," Falconi replied. He reached out and was given Riley's beer. "The fourth is one of the Algerians. We're sending him in to the Agency for a possible ID."

Blue Richards leaped to the ground. "He was a crazy-assed camel jockey that come a-runnin' at us, yellin' weird shit. So we blowed the motherfucker away." He waited for Calvin Culpepper to join him. The black demo sergeant nodded a greeting to Fagin, then he and Blue went on off the pad without pausing.

"Who bought it?" Fagin asked, checking the other detachment members as they unassed the H34 and followed Blue back toward their bunker.

"The two new guys—Bernstein and Taylor," Falconi answered dully. "And Kim."

"Kim!" Fagin bit his lip. "Damn!"

"Not too surprising when you get a bunch of guys in a situation where they're cut off and badly outnumbered," Falconi said coldly.

"I didn't write that OPLAN," Fagin argued.

"I'll bet you didn't protest it much though," Falconi said.

Top Gordon and Ray Swift Elk wordlessly walked past them toward the bunker. Chief Brewster, Chris Hawkins and Hank Valverde quickly followed. Malpractice McCorckel was the last man. He called out after his friends:

"Hey! Don't you silly fuckers drink any cold beer too

fast. Sip it slow or you'll just get sicker'n hell and cause a lot of extra work for me." He glanced over at the CIA man. "Hi, Fagin."

Fagin gave a little wave at the departing medic. "Well! One of you fuckers finally said hello to me."

Archie Dobbs and Stensland joined Falconi, Fagin and Riley. Archie, who had learned about Kim's death over the radio, was not particularly cheerful. "Are we gonna get a chaplain for the dead guys?"

"We'd need three, Archie," Falconi said. "A Buddhist for Kim, a rabbi for Bernstein and a Protestant for Taylor."

"I see," Archie said. "It'd be kinda unfair to slight one of 'em, huh?"

"Yeah. Let's get together over at the bunker and remember 'em in our own way," Falconi said.

"If it's any consolation," Fagin said, "the mission was a success. The Commies have been properly discouraged from turning their struggle here into an international event."

Falconi shrugged. "A mission is a mission, Fagin. I don't give a damn if we put a stop to that plan, or pounded the Russian army into hamburger. I lost three guys. That's what's on my mind right now."

Archie didn't like the mood. He decided to brighten it. "Hey, Skipper. I forgot to tell you. Major Riley says you owe him a beer."

Riley grinned. "That's right, goddamnit!"

"C'mon, I'll get one outta the fridge," Falconi said. He glanced over at Fagin. "I dump on you a lot, but I know where your heart really is."

"Yeah?" Fagin said sourly.

Archie clapped Fagin on the shoulder. "That's the Falcon's way of inviting you over for beer, Chuck."

Fagin sneered. "Don't get fond of me, shithead."

Falconi and Archie turned and walked toward their

bunker. Riley glanced at Fagin. "It's not a good idea to get too close to guys you send out to die."

Fagin bit his lower lip and glanced over at the chopper where the dead lie. "It tears your guts out, man."

Falconi, who had heard the exchange, turned back. "Hey, Fagin! Nobody said this job was going to be easy."

Archie called back too. "Whataya say, Chuck? You coming over for a beer?"

"You're goddamned right! I'm gonna drink every fucking beer in that fucking refrigerator of yours — you bastards!"

The four men strode rapidly across Nui Dep toward a few hours of forgetfulness.

# Epilogue

The small hamlet of Tam Nuroc was nestled on a curving bank of the Song Cai River. Breezes, cooled by the water, made it a lush, refreshing oasis in the steaming jungle. The village huts, situated in a palm grove, were twenty meters from the river itself. A small dock, constructed of lashed tree logs, projected out into deeper water so that the larger boats that traveled the waterway could tie up there during visits to the little town.

Tam Nuroc had always been primarily a marketplace. Countless generations of Vietnamese country people gathered there for animated bargaining, important meetings, politics and social events. Trading, selling, employment and even arrangements of marriages had flourished in the village square for as long as anyone could remember.

But for a period of time, Tam Nuroc played a different role. It still served as a central meeting place, but the friendliness and joviality were no longer in evidence during those long months. The villagers became members of a self-defense militia who were forced to turn to weapons in order to defend themselves against attacks of the Viet Cong.

When the Communists established themselves in the area, they could not tolerate such displays of free

222

enterprise in the countryside. Particularly if it actually benefited everyone concerned. After several murderous raids on their village by the Viet Cong, the people had turned to the government for help, and their militia was formed. An effective training program, and American supplied equipment, had produced a force strong enough to not only resist the Red encroachment into their lives, but to actually defeat the local Viet Cong company and rid the countryside of the dangerous pests.

But the victory, and two years of peace, eventually made the villagers complacent. Then, unfortunately, things came to a head during the big market day that celebrated the holiday of the Feast of Doan Ngo.

The river bank was packed with people, their customary dealings carried out in a loud combination of chattering and laughter. The sound of the approaching patrol boat scarcely attracted their attention. ARVN river units frequently called on Tam Nuroc during these occasions so the men could buy food to supplement their rations.

An old man, standing behind his boiling pot of noodle soup, anxiously waited for the soldiers to come ashore. They always purchased canteen cups of his delicacy, and paid good piasters for it too. But something troubled him as he watched the boat ease toward the shore. The men in it were military, no doubt, but the two heavy machine guns mounted on the flying bridge were aimed straight into the crowd.

Then he saw the red stars on the gunners' pith helmets.

Before the oldster could shout an alarm, the automatic weapons kicked into action. The slugs sprayed into the compact crowd, crashing into the marketeers and mowing them down in screaming packs.

The killing went on for fifteen minutes, and included

two reloads of 250-round belts, before the boat's motor was thrown into reverse. The coxswain backed the craft out into deeper water, then turned the bow toward the north. He hit the throttles hard and roared back up the river.

The days of peace were gone, not only for Tam Nuroc, but for the whole of the Song Cai River.